STORM OF EON

EON WARRIORS #7

ANNA HACKETT

Storm of Eon

Published by Anna Hackett

Copyright 2020 by Anna Hackett

Cover by Melody Simmons of BookCoversCre8tive

Edits by Tanya Saari

ISBN (ebook): 978-1-922414-19-9

ISBN (paperback): 978-1-922414-20-5

At Star's End – One of Library Journal's Best E-Original Romances for 2014

The Phoenix Adventures – SFR Galaxy Award Winner for Most Fun New Series and "Why Isn't This a Movie?" Series

Beneath a Trojan Moon – SFR Galaxy Award Winner and RWAus Ella Award Winner

Hell Squad – SFR Galaxy Award for best Post-Apocalypse for Readers who don't like Post-Apocalypse

"Like Indiana Jones meets Star Wars. A treasure hunt with a steamy romance." – SFF Dragon, review of *Among Galactic Ruins*

"Action, danger, aliens, romance – yup, it's another great book from Anna Hackett!" – Book Gannet Reviews, review of *Hell Squad: Marcus*

Sign up for my VIP mailing list and get your *free box set* containing three action-packed romances.

Visit here to get started: www.annahackett.com

CHAPTER ONE

U gh, this was really annoying.

Dr. Finley Delgado stepped out of Space Corps Headquarters and into the warm Houston day. She blinked at the sunlight, fighting her bad mood about having to leave her lab and her work.

She huffed out a breath and headed toward the crowd gathered on the lawn. A dais was set up, along with rows of chairs. The hum of conversation was loud as people talked, clearly excited.

All this pomp and circumstance to welcome some brawny alien warriors to Earth.

Finley stayed near the edge of the crowd. If she ventured much closer, she'd have to talk to someone.

All she wanted was to be in her lab, working on her project. Her really important project. Her gaze drifted over the buildings that made up Space Corps Headquarters. An old SpaceX rocket sat on display. It was a far cry from what the Space Corps fleet of starships looked like today.

Then her gaze snagged on the ruined building in the distance, partly collapsed and fenced off. Scorch marks covered the walls.

She swallowed, and remembered the attack six days ago. She'd been evacuated with the other scientists. They'd huddled together in a bomb shelter beneath the building, while a Kantos strike team had done its best to blow up Space Corps.

The Kantos.

Finley's chest tightened, like it had filled with concrete. The insectoid aliens had set their sights on Earth—to destroy the planet, and consume humans as food. She winced at the thought of being some bug's entree.

"This is exciting, isn't it?" A bubbly, blonde scientist from microbiology bopped over to Finley. Her name was Aimee and the woman bopped everywhere, all perky and happy. The woman could talk, talk, and talk. Finley routinely avoided her.

"What's exciting?" Finley asked.

Aimee rolled her big, blue eyes. "The Eon warriors arriving." The woman bounced on her feet and Finley resisted the urge to pat the woman's head like she was an overexcited puppy.

"I find it more inconvenient than exciting."

"Finley," the woman said, clearly exasperated. "They're Eon warriors!"

Another alien species, now allied with Earth. The Eon were big and brawny, with warships and advanced technology, and were helping Earth fight the Kantos.

Finley grunted. "They'll just be disruptive and get in

my way." She *really* wanted to get back to her lab. She glanced at the ruined building again. Her still-experimental defense weapon—the StarStorm—had been used as a last resort, and had repelled the Kantos strike team and destroyed their ship. The weapon was nowhere near finished yet, and there were bugs—the non-Kantos kind—in the targeting system. Space Corps were damn lucky they hadn't razed Houston to the ground when they'd risked using it.

She was still working on the ground-defense part of the StarStorm, and needed to refine the targeting. Once that was done, they'd move onto orbital testing. Once she finished, Earth would have an orbital defense net that would provide security to the entire planet.

"They can help us," Aimee insisted.

Finley made an unconvinced sound. *Right.* The Eon had advanced technology, but the warrior who'd called her prior to this trip had been big and muscular, and likely spent more time in the gym than the lab.

She wanted their tech, not their warriors.

"Well, I'm going to get to know them." Aimee fluffed her hair.

Finley watched the move. Did hair fluffing make any difference to her attractiveness? Finley's hair was tamed into a braid so it would stay out of her way.

"The Eon are hunky. Total fantasy material." Aimee got a dreamy look in her eye. "Several are mated to humans now."

Ugh. Finley had heard that a colleague of hers, Wren Traynor, had mated with an Eon war commander. Her sisters were mated to other warriors, as well. So strange. Wren had always seemed reasonably intelligent.

Men were mostly a waste of time, in Finley's opinion.

"Let's get a drink." Aimee suggested.

"Fine." Finley attempted to shake off her bad mood. They moved closer to the crowd, and she nodded at Admiral Linda Barber, one of the top brass at Space Corps.

Then, she spotted a crying woman and several families. A man was clutching a small child to his chest and talking with a Space Corps official dressed in a neatly-pressed uniform.

Finley froze. The mother's sobbing drilled into Finley's head. For a second, she was thrown back in time. To another woman's harsh sobs. To pain, darkness, and despair.

She couldn't breathe.

"It's so sad," Aimee whispered. "That family was touring HQ when the Kantos attacked. Their eighteen-year-old son died."

Finley felt a rock lodge in her gut. She remembered another young man, a math prodigy, who'd also been killed.

All because Finley hadn't been smart enough, fast enough, or courageous enough.

"Your weapon stopped the attack, Finley," Aimee continued. "It saved lives."

Just not soon enough.

Crushing guilt was a familiar sensation. She tried to drag in a breath, but it was so hard to breathe. She grabbed the elastic band she kept on her wrist and snapped it. The sting on her skin felt like a lifeline.

Then she heard a whoosh of sound overhead.

Like the rest of the gathering, she looked up and gasped.

The sleek, black shuttle had blue lights along the side. It was so streamlined and aerodynamic.

"They're here," Aimee said breathlessly.

The Eon shuttle was a fine piece of design. The weapons scientist in Finley wondered what weapons capabilities it had.

The starship touched down on the landing pad nearby, and moments later, the side door slid smoothly open.

Three Eon warriors disembarked.

At first glance, they all looked the same. Tall, broad shouldered, with muscular bodies clad in black uniforms. Their shirts had no sleeves, so there were lots of muscles on display.

Beside Finley, Aimee made a sound that sounded suspiciously like a moan.

The warriors all had long, brown hair, and rugged faces. Two had hair close to their shoulders, in a lighter shade of brown.

The third one...

Finley stiffened, and felt an odd, electric shock zing through her body. It was him. The one she'd met on the call.

Security Commander Sabin Solann-Ath.

His hair was a shade darker than the others—a deep, oak-brown—and slightly shorter, too. He stood a little straighter, and projected a sense of power and strength. Like he'd pick up a sword and shield and charge into battle to protect his princess.

Jesus. Finley shook her head. See, Eon warriors were a huge distraction. She pulled her unruly mind and body back into line.

Space Corps officials moved forward to welcome the warriors. These three men were allegedly all Eon weapons experts.

Solann-Ath lifted his head and their gazes met. Finley blinked and her heart did something weird. Maybe she was coming down with something?

His eyes were almost pure black, but they were threaded with impossibly beautiful strands of purple. She saw a flash of recognition on his face.

His gaze slid over her body and she tensed.

She knew what he saw—an almost-six-foot-tall woman, with more curves than were fashionable, wearing ordinary clothes and a lab coat.

For a horrible second, it dredged up memories of the quarterback she'd dated briefly in high school. He'd called her a beautiful Amazon, but after taking her virginity, he'd called her an unattractive giant.

She really must be coming down with something.

Finley lifted her chin and glared at the Eon warrior, then she turned away.

SO FAR, Sabin didn't see much about Earth to excite him.

He did appreciate the green vegetation, the clear, blue sky, and the fresh air. The sunlight was warm on his skin. He took a second to absorb it all. It made a nice change to being aboard a warship.

His helian symbiont, housed snugly in the thick band on his wrist, pulsed. The buildings in the city appeared to be an irregular mix of different construction.

Ahead, a crowd waited for them.

"Well, warriors, this is our home for the foreseeable future," Security Commander Rade Vann-Felis said. The warrior was from the science ship, the *Solent*. The other warrior, Gadon Harann-Jad was a scientist from the Eon planet Ath.

Sabin scanned the area, taking in the partly destroyed building. His jaw tightened. That would have been from the recent attack. They had to stop the Kantos, or they'd annihilate Earth, then go after the Eon.

Several Space Corps officers, wearing navy-blue uniforms, stepped forward to greet them. But Sabin looked past them and spotted a tall woman in a white coat. She was staring at him boldly. The coat draped her magnificent figure.

Dr. Finley Delgado. He perused the woman he'd be working with, then she gave him another bold look before she looked away.

His pulse spiked.

"Welcome, I'm Admiral Linda Barber."

Sabin focused on the woman in front of him and shook hands with the admiral. She looked to be several decades older than Sabin, her ash-colored hair in a sleek cut to her jaw line. Her brown gaze was direct and steady.

"Admiral, I'm Security Commander Sabin Solann-Ath of the *Rengard*."

"A pleasure, Security Commander. Ambassador Thann-Eon has kept us updated on all the assistance you, your war commander, and your ship have been giving us. Thank you."

He inclined his head. This woman was more welcoming than her scientist. "The Kantos are our shared enemy. We will do whatever is necessary to stop them."

"Thank you. We hope your stay here is beneficial and fruitful."

Another man moved up beside the general. He was maybe ten years older than Sabin. "I'm Dr. Eli Kemp, head of Space Corps Projects. Allow me to introduce you to the scientist in charge of the StarStorm Project, who you'll be paired with for your time here."

"Thank you." Sabin noted the other warriors had been led away by other Space Corps officers. Dr. Kemp led Sabin toward Finley Delgado.

"Security Commander, meet Dr. Delgado. Finley, this is—"

"Security Commander Sabin Solann-Ath." She held out her hand, her gaze direct. "I read the report."

He shook it, wrapping his fingers around hers and saw the faintest flush in her cheeks. Her hand squeezed his. Her hair was golden, several shades lighter than it had appeared on their call.

Unlike some other Terran women, who were downright tiny, she was tall and strong. Her scent hit him—subtle, with a mix of spicy and sweet notes.

"I'll leave you to it." With a nod, Kemp left them.

"I look forward to working with you on the StarStorm weapons system," Sabin said.

Dr. Delgado sniffed. "Security Commander, as I told you, I don't need help."

He cocked his head. "My species is technologically advanced compared to yours."

Her brown eyes flashed. "I know, but we understand our planet better than you do. I would like access to your technology, but not to have you—" her gaze drifted across his chest "—poking around in my research and slowing me down."

A spurt of anger, amplified by his helian, made Sabin grit his teeth. "Perhaps I could speed up your work."

"I doubt that."

"You're very arrogant," he said.

Her eyes widened, her voice a low hiss. "I'm the renowned expert on Terran laser weapons systems. Just because I don't like people dictating who I work with and who gets access to my project, doesn't mean I'm arrogant. I simply state facts, and I'm direct. I don't—" she blew out a breath "—know how to play polite games."

Hmm, he was starting to see another side to the scientist. Sabin didn't mind it when people were direct and said what they meant. "I don't like games, either."

"I'm glad to hear that, Security Commander."

"Call me Sabin. We'll be working closely together, so we should dispense with the titles."

Her nose wrinkled. "Fine. Finley."

"Finley." He liked her name.

More color touched her cheeks. "I hope you'll stay out of my way while you're here."

Well, that cease-fire hadn't lasted long. "I'll do whatever is required to stop the Kantos."

"I guess we have that goal in common, at least." Her gaze shifted.

He saw her looking where some families were gathered. A sobbing woman was leaning into a man.

"Victims and families of the recent attack," Finley said. "I won't let more kids die." She spun and stalked away, her long legs eating up the ground. She disappeared inside the building.

Well, the woman wasn't pleasant, and she was opinionated, but he was told she was good at what she did.

And like she said, they shared a common goal.

He scanned the Space Corps grounds again.

His family had all called him before he'd left for Earth, thrilled at the honor given to him by the king of the Eon Empire.

They were a warrior family—his father and mother were both warriors. His two brothers were warriors. Sabin had never been given a choice. He was fit, athletic, and strategically minded. From birth, he'd been well-suited to becoming a warrior.

If he'd ever felt yearnings for...more, well, he never gave into them.

The scent of Finley taunted his senses. He savored it. It flared along his senses, along with the feel of the hot sun, the murmur of the crowd.

His chest tightened. No, he would not let distractions get in the way. He would stay focused on his task.

The sooner he got to work, the better.

"Security Commander?" A young Space Corps officer stood nearby. "Allow me to show you to your quarters."

The man led Sabin into the main building. An elevator took them up several levels, and he was shown into some neat rooms—with a kitchenette in the corner, a living area, and an adjoining large bedroom and bathroom.

"We worked hard with our chef to provide food that will be pleasing to your Eon palate."

"Thank you."

"Anything else? I'm sure you want to rest after your journey."

"Actually, I want to get to work."

The man blinked.

"Can you tell me where to find Dr. Delgado's lab?"

The man winced. "Devil Delgado."

"Excuse me?" Sabin frowned.

"That's what people call her. Dr. Delgado can be...difficult."

"Is she good at her work?"

"A genius with weapons systems. And no one works harder."

Sabin nodded. "That's all I need to know."

"Well, be warned. She doesn't work well with others, and she hates people in her lab."

"I can handle the doctor. Where's her lab?"

"Lowest-level. Lab B5."

"Thank you." Sabin strode out, following the signs to the elevators and down to Finley's lab.

He was eager to get to work.

And strangely, he was eager to cross paths with the prickly doctor again.

CHAPTER TWO

Finley pushed herself away from her computer and slumped back in her chair. Usually, her lab was her calm space, where she could focus.

Instead, she was distracted. She glanced at the computer screen. All the calculations and simulations were starting to blur.

She had to fix this problem in the targeting system, but she couldn't damn well find the culprit. It had to be right before they could start any ground testing of the lasers, let alone orbital testing.

But her focus was scattered.

By a big, hard-to-ignore, Eon warrior.

She let out a low growl and closed her eyes. She tried a little meditation. She'd always had a hard time relaxing, even as a little girl. Her family was all normal. Normal parents. Normal siblings. Her sports-loving brothers were popular and outgoing. She was the odd one out. Her family loved her, but didn't understand her. They'd always had a hard time keeping her stimulated. She'd skipped several years of school, but not too many. Her parents hadn't wanted her to be a thirteen-year-old college student.

Finley had tried to fit in at school, but she'd eventually given up. She wasn't friendly and smiling like all the other girls. She'd just spent all her time studying harder.

Then, as a young, twenty-four-year-old attending a conference in Africa, she and two of her colleagues had been abducted by a terrorist group.

Nausea swirled and she opened her eyes. Why was she even thinking about this? Her nightmares had stopped long ago, and the panic attacks were rare. Sabin was to blame for that, as well.

It was those eyes of his.

"Well, it's no wonder you need help if you sit in your lab staring at the wall."

Finley started, and her head whipped around.

Sabin stood in the doorway, his massive shoulders almost brushing the sides of it.

She scowled. "I was thinking."

He wandered in and made a noncommittal sound.

"I asked you not to get in my way," she said.

"You remind me of a *garva*."

"What's that?"

"A bad-tempered, little creature covered in armor from my homeworld of Ath. It sprays poison when threatened."

Her gaze narrowed. "Are we going to trade insults?"

He smiled. "That wasn't an insult. I like *garvas*. I had one as a pet when I was young."

"Warrior—"

"*Sabin.*" He walked along one of the long benches in her lab, then paused. "You have a scale model of your weapons system."

"Yes." She blew out a breath. "Sometimes I find it better to imagine things in real life, not just simulations on the computer screen. That shows the design for the StarStorm satellites. They each have a solar array for power, and are equipped with lasers. If a Kantos ship approaches, we can activate the StarStorm array, and it will create an impenetrable net around the Earth. One deadly to Kantos ships. The satellites are still being built, and we need to keep testing the lasers on the ground before we head into space. I...have a few problems with the targeting system. It needs to be more precise."

Sabin nodded. "I'd like to learn everything I can about the project."

Finley crossed her arms. "I don't have time to—"

"Make time. I can help, Finley. You want to protect your planet, right?"

"Of course. I just can't stop my work though." She grabbed a tablet off the bench and slapped it against his chest. The man was rock hard. "All the data on the project is on that. Don't lose it, because it's classified."

One of his big hands circled her wrist. She suddenly realized they were standing awfully close. He was so big. She wasn't used to feeling small and looking up at a man.

"Your heart rate increased," he said.

She frowned. "What?" *He could tell?*

"I have enhanced senses."

Her gaze dropped to his thick wrist, and the black band surrounding it. "Because of your helian."

She had to admit, she was fascinated by the alien symbiont. She couldn't imagine being joined to a creature that gave you increased strength and enhanced senses, and allowed you to generate armor and weapons with a thought.

"Yes," he replied.

She yanked on her hand, and he released her.

He looked back at her model of the weapons system, and Finley turned back to her computer. Her simulations were still running.

Damn. She needed to get busy with something, so he'd leave. She grabbed a screwdriver. She'd been meaning to adjust the test laser casing.

She moved to the bulky unit and started adjusting the screws.

"I can help with the targeting systems," he said. "That's a specialty of mine. Maybe we can find a way to blend Eon technology with your Terran tech."

His deep voice, right behind her, made her jerk. Her finger slipped, and she gashed it on the metal.

"*Ow.*" The screwdriver clattered to the bench and she stuck her finger in her mouth, the iron taste of blood on her tongue.

Sabin spun her. "Let me see."

"It's just a scratch."

"I can smell the blood, Finley." He grabbed her hand.

They indulged in a brief game of tug-of-war. His hands were big, strong, and warm. Finley felt a strange tingle in her belly.

Oh God, no.

He pulled her hand close.

16

"You have an ugly little cut on your finger." He stroked her skin, and every single one of her senses flared to life.

No, no, no. She couldn't be attracted to this man. That would be a massive problem.

"I have a first aid kit somewhere," she said. "I'll take care of it later." Her pulse skittered. She needed to get away from him.

"I have a better idea." He pulled something off his belt. He lifted a small vial that contained red fluid.

"What's that?"

"*Havv.* A healing fluid infused with bio-organisms similar to my helian."

He gently squeezed a drop on her cut and then smoothed it over her skin. Finley felt the stroke of his fingers, the pulse of heat deep in her belly and shockingly, between her legs.

She licked her lips. She was unequipped to deal with this. She'd had sex a few times in her life, and it hadn't been great. She certainly never felt the need to go back for more. And she'd never felt this hot, vicious attraction to anyone before.

Pull yourself together, Finley.

Sabin's head shot up, his gaze on her face. He'd gone still, like a predator sensing prey.

She tried not to blush. The man noticed too many details.

She tugged her hand out of his and realized that the cut was all healed.

"Wow, that's incredible." There wasn't a mark left on her skin. "What level of injury can it heal?"

He was still staring at her.

"Sabin?"

He shook his head and blinked.

"The *havv*," she said again. "What kind of injuries can it heal?"

He cleared his throat. "Significant. See, perhaps I can help you."

"Maybe. Now go and do your reading." She made a shooing motion. "Get up to speed on the project."

"I'll see you later, Finley Delgado."

As soon as he left, she sagged against the bench. Why did those words seem like a threat? And why wasn't she more annoyed by it?

FROWNING, Sabin reentered his quarters.

Finley had responded to him. He'd sensed her pulse spike, detected the flush in her cheeks, and smelled the faint bite of her arousal. The scientist put up a good façade of surliness and disinterest, but Sabin sensed there was more to her.

And his own body had responded, as well.

Even now, desire was a hard pulse in his gut, amplified by his helian. He'd stood there, touching her hand, his senses filled with her unique scent that seemed designed just for him, and he'd wanted more.

He wanted to get to know her better. Something told him that Dr. Delgado didn't show her real self very much.

Devil Delgado. He frowned at the moniker. How

many people treated her with disrespect and didn't understand her?

He set the tablet down on the table. Not that he would act on this attraction. Control was the cornerstone of Sabin's life. It was important to a warrior, but he had an even more personal reason to keep a tight grip on his control.

Against his will, his thoughts turned to Finley. Her scent, her looks, her intelligence—she was far too appealing. And he wasn't here to tame a cranky scientist, or indulge in personal relationships.

He had a job to do.

Kantos to repel.

Lives to save.

He sat at the table and pulled out his communicator. It was the Eon version of the tablet.

A spike from his helian snaked out and interfaced into the device, and with a flicker of a thought, he made the call.

A moment later, his war commander's face appeared. Malax Dann-Jad was sitting in his office aboard the *Rengard*, lights on low behind him.

"It's late," Sabin said. "Sorry, Malax."

"It's fine, Sabin. Wren's sleeping, and I didn't want to wake her. You made it safely to Earth?"

"Yes. I'm at Space Corps Headquarters."

Malax shifted. He was bare chested, and had clearly risen from his bed to take the call. "You met Dr. Delgado?"

"Yes."

The war commander cocked his head. "Is she as difficult as Wren's told me?"

"Yes, but it won't stop us working together. She might be difficult, but she's straightforward. And clearly intelligent."

Malax nodded. "We need that weapons system up and running. The Kantos are getting bolder."

"Or more desperate."

"They want Earth, Sabin. They want to annihilate it and its people. We won't let that happen."

Malax was a warrior to the core, driven to protect the innocent. And Sabin knew that he loved his Terran mate. He wouldn't let his mate's planet be destroyed.

"How are Airen and Donovan?" Sabin asked.

The war commander's lips twitched. "The Terran certainly keeps Airen on her toes. And they work well together. She's happy. More relaxed."

"Good." The second commander deserved some happiness with her new mate.

Malax's face turned serious. "Sabin, Kantos ships were spotted near Landa Prime."

Sabin frowned. That wasn't far from Earth's solar system. "How many?"

"Two battle cruisers."

Not many, but Sabin's thoughts ticked over.

"Sabin, they could be amassing a small invasion fleet."

That thought gave him a chill. The Kantos had to be stopped. He thought of the crying family he'd seen earlier. "I'll put everything I have into getting Dr. Delgado's weapon system operational."

"I know you will. Good luck, and keep me informed."
Sabin nodded.

The screen went black, and Sabin made another call.

A warrior's face appeared. He was leaner than Sabin, his brown hair threaded with gray. Some of it had been earned by age and experience, but Medical Commander Thane Kann-Eon had gone gray earlier than normal for an Eon warrior.

"Sabin." His friend smiled. "How's Earth?"

"Warm. Fragrant. The air's fresher than what the recyclers give us on the *Rengard*."

"I know your senses are extra acute; are you handling it okay?"

"I'm fine."

Thane was one of the few people who knew that Sabin suffered from a condition of extrasensory perception. How he and his helian had bonded meant that Sabin was able to pick up even more with his senses than most warriors. He heard more, smelled more acutely, had better vision. He even felt more.

"How's your scientist?" Thane asked.

Gorgeous and smells irresistible. "Pricklier than a *garva*, but I'm told that she's highly competent."

Thane laughed. "I thought maybe you'd end up with a friendly Terran, perhaps even your mate."

Sabin forced a laugh. "I won't ever have a mate."

Every warrior wondered what having a mate would be like. Sabin had wondered. Especially since he'd watched Malax and Wren, and now Airen and Donovan mate.

To have your helian accept another person...

No, it would be a risk that Sabin wouldn't ever take.

Having a mate to indulge all his senses in... With his extrasensory abilities, he was always tempted to immerse himself in so many pleasurable things. On the rare times he shared sex with a woman, he kept the interactions brief and controlled. He couldn't risk losing his control. Losing himself.

He ruthlessly kept his needs and desires in check. He wouldn't follow the same path as his uncle.

Sabin's gut clenched. His father's brother had descended into ruin, then worse.

There would be no mate for Sabin. Ever.

"Sabin?"

He blinked back at Thane's concerned face.

"You're thinking of your uncle. You *aren't* him."

Thane was both a medical commander and friend, and knew Sabin's family history.

"We both have the same overdeveloped senses. One slip, and I could be him."

"You're a warrior. You're too disciplined to ever fall like he did."

His uncle Varlan hadn't been a warrior, but he'd once been a respected engineer. Until he'd lost himself in *sotora*.

Sotora was a potent, fragrant scent drug. His uncle had spent so much time high on *sotora* that he'd hurt people, taken a mate and then neglected her, shamed his family, and eventually died from an overdose.

Sabin would *not* bring shame to his family.

"You're allowed pleasure, Sabin," Thane said. "Denying yourself is just as bad as overindulging."

22

Sabin thought for a second of indulging in Finley Delgado. What sounds would she make when he pleasured her? How soft was her skin—on her belly, behind her knee, at her inner thighs?

Sabin's cock throbbed, lengthening. He stifled a groan.

"I guess it's a good thing that your doctor is difficult," Thane said. "No temptation there."

"Yes. Right." Never mind the fact that she was tall, well-built, with hair like gold.

Thane smiled. "Well, I wish you good luck."

"Thanks, Thane. I need this weapons system operational before the Kantos return. They *will* come back."

"No doubt about it. Good luck, Sabin."

He suspected he'd need it.

CHAPTER THREE

R ubbing her eyes, Finley fought back a yawn.

It was really late. Outside was dark, and she only had a few lights on in the lab. The glow from her computer screen washed her in blue.

Everything on the screen was a blur. She leaned back and her chair squeaked. She reached for her weakness—marshmallows. She always kept some in her lab. She popped the soft sweetness in her mouth. Then another.

In her head, she kept seeing that distraught family, thinking of the boy who died. The marshmallows turned to dust.

It all reminded her of her week in captivity.

Her heart squeezed and she reached for the elastic on her wrist. The sting was a welcome pain.

The conference had been stimulating. She'd been friendlier then, more open. Brent had been a young math genius who'd graduated college early and joined Space Corps' Science Unit. Melody had been a year younger than Finley, with a specialty in lasers. They'd all been friends.

Then the terrorists had attacked.

They'd kept the three of them locked in a hole in the ground, only pulling them out to demand they create weapons for the group.

Finley had been defiant. Mostly because she'd been terrified. She'd kept telling the others that rescue would come. It finally had. Too late for Brent and Melody.

She gripped the edge of her desk and did her breathing exercises. Brent and Melody were her motivation for everything. Studying hard, working hard, staying focused on her task. She had to live and work for both of them. She had to ensure their deaths weren't in vain.

God. She pinched the bridge of her nose. She'd probably worked enough for tonight. She'd wanted to avoid the welcome dinner for the Eon warriors.

She snorted. Okay, truth be told, she'd wanted to avoid Sabin.

Heat washed over her and she reached up to flick open a couple of buttons of her shirt. She kicked off her shoes. With barely any effort she could picture him—big, muscular, that rugged face.

Jeez. She was clearly in lust. She dropped her head to the desk. The last thing she needed was an inconvenient attraction to an alien warrior.

Not that it mattered. She was well aware that she wasn't the kind of pretty, delicate, slender woman that men were attracted to. For some reason—like that jerk-off, football player ex—Finley was attracted to athletic men. *Damn hormones.*

She heard a sound and turned. She frowned. There was no one there.

Yep, she was getting tired.

She turned back to her computer and lifted a hand to massage the tense muscles at the back of her neck. She wondered where Sabin was. Probably sleeping. Then her unruly brain imagined him in bed. Naked.

Finley groaned and shifted her legs. Her skin was flushed, and the sensation of her thighs rubbing together made her bite her lip.

When she got back to her quarters, she needed to take a cold shower and then take care of herself. She gave herself better orgasms than any man ever had, anyway.

This was all the warrior's fault. She heard a sound again. Like something moving.

Finley slipped on her shoes and rose. It had better not be a mouse. She'd seen one the size of a small dog, once. She shuddered. She *hated* mice.

She grabbed her metal ruler off the desk, just in case she needed to shoo a rodent away. She crept along the bench, peering under it.

Nothing.

Then, a louder noise came from the hall, and she froze. That sounded like something big.

Heart pounding, Finley peeked around the doorway.

And squelched a scream. "Frank, you *scared* me."

The janitor with a mop and bucket was moving down the corridor. He had wireless earphones in but when he spotted her, the older man lifted a hand.

She waved back and turned.

Definitely time for bed.

She headed back to her computer and stopped to study her scale model. Tonight, she'd do something to get this irrational attraction to Sabin under control, then tomorrow, she'd work with the warrior.

Getting this weapons system operational was her only priority.

She turned and tripped over a stool, going down on her hands and knees. *Jesus.* She wasn't usually this clumsy.

She lifted her head and froze.

The creature was crouched under the bench, directly at eye level. It had a long, humanoid form, covered in black, leathery skin. Its protracted limbs were folded in, its wings pulled around itself.

Its face was dominated by bug eyes—loads of them. It cocked its head, and she saw her own reflection in the silvery sheen.

Finley tried to swallow, her mouth dry.

Then with a screech, the alien flew at her.

She screamed.

The creature barreled at her and when it hit, it knocked her flat. The damn thing was heavier than it looked.

As Finley stared, wide-eyed, the alien opened its mouth. A protuberance extended out of the center of its mouth, and stretched toward her face, drool dripping off it.

Oh. *God.*

She twisted and tried to shove the thing off her. It had her pinned down, and she couldn't move. Claws pricked painfully into her chest.

She screamed again. Damn, would Frank even hear her over his music? The rest of the building's labs were empty, and the living quarters were all on the upper levels. No one would hear her scream.

Or hear her die a horrible, bloody death.

The alien's face was getting closer, the protuberance aimed for her eye. Drool dripped onto her cheek and stung.

She reached out her hand, scrabbling to try and find anything. Her fingers closed on cool metal.

The stool.

She grabbed it and yanked.

It slammed into the creature's head. The alien screeched and fell off her with a cry. Finley rolled onto her knees and scrambled to her feet. She ran, sprinting between two benches.

Sabin. She had to get to Sabin. He could stop it.

She sprinted for the door.

The alien leaped, and hit the bench beside her, knocking equipment to the floor with a loud crash. Swallowing a scream, Finley stumbled back.

The alien snapped its wings out. They were batlike, the tips of them covered in sharp barbs. It swiped a claw at her.

She ducked and felt a sting across her back. She scrambled under one of the benches.

She had to get to the door.

With a wild screech, the alien hit the floor between the benches.

Finley stayed crouched, and moved as fast as she could. The alien slammed into another bench, sending it

28

sliding. Her model crashed to the floor, pieces rolling everywhere.

Finley lifted her head and her heart knocked against her ribs.

The damn thing was between her and the door.

Those bug eyes locked on her.

Its mouth gaped open and the protuberance reappeared. It reminded her of something out of a horror movie. Finley could barely think over the fear drumming through her.

"You are *really* ugly." She grabbed a box off the closest bench.

The alien flew at her. She threw the box and screamed.

SABIN WOKE FROM A LIGHT SLEEP. He never slept well in a new location, until he acclimated to sleeping off-ship. He'd gotten far too used to the stillness of space flight, and the gentle whoosh of air recyclers.

He scanned his Space Corps quarters. The room was shadowed. Quiet.

What had woken him?

He heard a faint, furtive sound.

He pushed the sheets off. He was only wearing tight, black undershorts. His helian throbbed.

Yes, I sense it, too.

He opened his senses. *There.* There was something in his closet.

Scales flickered over his body, flowing from the helian

band to cover his arm, then across his chest and the rest of his body. Once his armor was in place, he snatched up his utility belt from the side table and clipped it on. Then he morphed a short sword that had a faint purple glow.

He yanked open the closet door.

A bug sprang out.

It was the size of a hunting dog. A mottled brown-and-black in color, it had a long body, with a narrow head, six sturdy legs, and a row of spikes along its back.

Sabin slashed with his sword. The bug dodged sideways, extremely agile. The spikes on its back vibrated, like it was picking up movements in the air.

The creature leaped onto a side table, sending a lamp crashing to the floor.

Sabin chased the alien into the living area. With two long strides, he stabbed with his sword, skewering the Kantos bug. Green blood sprayed onto the carpet and he pulled the sword back.

It was an ugly creature. He hadn't seen it before, but he knew it was Kantos. They bred all kinds of abominations.

He found his communicator and called Gadon and Rade. The other warriors had both clearly been sleeping, but snapped to alertness when he told them of the attack. They both checked their quarters and confirmed no sign of any Kantos.

Sabin made another call.

"Shouldn't you be sleeping?" Airen Kann-Felis' face appeared on screen. The second-in-command of the *Rengard* always looked prepared for anything.

"I was, but I had an uninvited visitor."

"A cute Earth woman?" Donovan asked from behind Airen.

The dark-skinned Terran Space Corps officer was extremely competent, and had been seconded to work aboard the *Rengard*. Sabin liked and respected the man.

"Unfortunately, not." Sabin turned the communicator so they could see the alien.

Airen made an unhappy sound.

Donovan whistled. "Ugly critter."

"The Kantos clearly know myself and the other warriors are here."

"Were the others attacked?" Airen asked.

"No."

"I got a pop in the Kantos database." Donovan frowned. "It's a stalker. Said to be a hunting bug that accompanies these guys." An image popped up on the screen.

Sabin's blood chilled. He took in the black skin, the wings. "That's a Kantos assassin."

Airen's brow creased. "If the bug came after you, who did the assassin go after?"

Sabin felt a pressure in his chest. "*Finley.*"

He dropped the communicator and ran.

He powered down the hall and hit the stairs. He thundered down several levels, sprinting toward her lab.

In his gut, he knew she'd still be there.

He sprinted past a startled man with a mop and a bucket. He rounded a corner and heard a screech in the distance. He made out the sound of a fight, and something crashing.

No.

Sabin charged into Finley's lab.

The Kantos assassin lifted her like she weighed nothing. It had one clawed hand wrapped around her neck. She twisted and jerked.

Sabin's sword lengthened, and he leaped over an overturned bench.

Finley saw him, her eyes widening.

Then she punched the Kantos in the eyes.

It tossed her, and she hit the wall and slid to the floor.

The creature spun and saw Sabin. Its wings snapped open, and it threw its bony arms wide.

Sabin swung his sword and the Kantos dodged, then it took flight, fluttering close to the ceiling.

Gritting his teeth, Sabin followed. He swung again, then spun and slashed.

He scored the alien's wing and it let out a deafening screech, crashing to the floor.

It flew at Sabin in a flurry of claws and flapping, barbed wings. He felt sharp talons scratch at his armor. A wash of energy flared from his helian. His armor was holding.

Jaws snapped at him and he stumbled back...and tripped.

Cren.

Sabin fell onto his back, his sword arm pinned by the creature.

"Get off him, you ugly asshole!"

Finley appeared, a bulky piece of equipment in her hands. She raised it over her head and then slammed it down on the back of the assassin's head.

The creature jerked and its hold loosened. Finley smashed it again.

Sabin heaved up and knocked the alien off him.

He grabbed Finley and shoved her behind him.

Swinging his sword, he stabbed down, slicing into the assassin. Its screech made Sabin wince, but he slashed again.

Finally, the Kantos slumped, its wings crumpled. Green blood pooled on the floor beneath it. The sharp stench of it swamped Sabin's senses.

Sabin turned.

Finley stared at the alien—her face white, her eyes wide. "God. *God.*" She pressed a hand to her stomach.

"Are you okay?" He detected her racing heart, her rapid breathing.

She dragged her gaze off the alien, and looked at him. Her face turned even whiter and she started to collapse, but Sabin's reflexes were fast.

He grabbed her and they both sank to the floor.

"I knew you would kill it." Her voice was shaky. "I was trying to get to you."

"Just take a deep breath. Hold on. You're okay."

He maneuvered her into his lap, his arms wrapped around her.

She let out a shuddering breath. "It was...terrifying."

"You're safe now."

With a sob, she pressed her face to his neck and held on. Her body shook and he felt a strange need to comfort her. He stroked her back and she clung tighter.

"Thank you," she said.

"You're welcome, Finley."

"I tried to get away." Her voice was shaky. "I knew you could kill it."

She'd held her own against a Kantos assassin and fought it when he needed help. There was a lot more to Dr. Finley Delgado. "You did well, Finley. Let me see your wounds." She had scratches on her face and on her chest. "I want to treat your scratches with *havv*."

He didn't tell her that the assassin could have poison on its claws.

She withdrew, and he watched as she pulled herself together. There were no tears, no hysterics. Her fingers toyed with a narrow band on her wrist, snapping it against her skin.

She was tough. Admiration hit his belly. There was an inner strength to Finley Delgado.

He pulled out his vial of *havv*. The scratches on her face weren't too deep, and he quickly smoothed the gel over them. Then he opened her shirt. He saw her pretty, pink underwear, then the red scratches on her skin. His body took notice of the smooth skin.

Not now, Sabin.

He started smoothing *havv* across the scratches, and his fingers brushed the top of her breast. Her chest hitched.

"Does it hurt?" *Just focus on her, nothing else.*

"No."

He looked at her face. It was flushed, her eyes bright.

"Finley? Are you all right?"

"Just grateful I'm alive, and not bleeding to death on my lab floor." She shot a quick glance at the assassin. "It's Kantos?"

"Yes."

She shuddered.

Sabin shifted her around so he could reach the scratch on her back. He finished with the *havv* and put the small vial away.

"There."

"I'm suddenly feeling quite glad that you were here, warrior." She touched his cheek and he felt that light touch all the way through his body. Their gazes met.

She had eyes of a deep, rich-brown color. He found it fascinating that her eyes were all one color, so unlike Eon eyes.

"Thank you for saving my life, Sabin."

Then she leaned forward and kissed him.

CHAPTER FOUR

F inley's brain short-circuited.

Sabin's lips were firm, warm. Except he wasn't kissing her back.

Oh, God. She was an idiot.

She was about to pull back, when his hands tightened on her and his mouth opened.

Then he *kissed* her.

His tongue was in her mouth, teasing hers. He tasted *so* good. Sensation shot through her like a wildfire.

She tilted her head and made a hungry sound.

An answering, masculine growl vibrated through Sabin. Finley thought she'd been kissed well before, and had always written it off as kind of boring.

Not now.

She leaned into him, and he tilted his head, his mouth slanting over hers. She couldn't think or breathe. She didn't want to think or breathe. All she wanted was to kiss Sabin Solann-Ath forever.

One of his strong hands slid into her hair. She'd lost

her hair tie in the fight and her hair was loose. He wrapped it around his fingers and tugged. Her head dropped back, and she felt a sweet sting in her scalp, and an answering tug between her legs.

His head lifted, his gaze on her. The purple strands in his eyes glowed brightly.

"You like that?" he asked, voice deep.

"Yes."

His hold on her hair tightened, and her lips parted.

"You're so strong," she murmured.

"I'd never hurt you."

"I know. That's what makes it so attractive."

He made a growling sound and kissed her again, nipping her lips. Then they were kissing each other senseless. Finley pressed closer.

Suddenly, there was a commotion in the hall. "Security!"

Oh, crap.

She pulled back and Sabin's eyes flashed. He rubbed his thumb over her bottom lip, which made her insides dance.

Then, he pulled her up off the floor with him.

"Here. I'm Security Commander Solann-Ath. We neutralized the threat."

The security team charged in—three men and one woman—guns in hand.

They took in the dead Kantos on the floor, and one of the men blanched. The woman stepped forward. She was only a few years older than Finley, and head of Space Corps Headquarters Security. Finley had admired Captain Alea Rodriguez since she'd met her. The captain was tall and athletic, and always in charge. The woman ran security with a firm, no-nonsense, and slightly scary hand.

The brunette's jaw firmed. "Lewis, organize a containment and cleanup crew."

"Yes, Captain."

Captain Rodriguez's light-brown gaze moved to where Finley stood in Sabin's arms. "Dr. Delgado, are you okay?"

"Thanks to Sabin." She shuddered.

The woman eyed the blood on Finley's lab coat. "The paramedics are on the way."

"I'm all right. Sabin dealt with my injuries." *And kissed my brains out.* Finley guessed the security captain didn't need to know that.

"I still want the paramedics to check you over." Rodriguez's tone warned Finley that she wasn't up for any arguments or negotiations.

"Fine," Finley muttered.

"Security Commander, I'm hoping I can get your statement." Rodriguez looked at the alien's body. "And your advice."

"There's another Kantos bug in my quarters," he said. "I killed it."

Finley gasped.

"Chen," Rodriguez barked. "Get a second team up to the security commander's quarters."

The man nodded. "On it, Captain."

Suddenly, hands spanned Finley's waist. With one move, Sabin lifted her onto a bench.

She gasped. One, no one's hands had ever spanned

her waist before, and two, no one could lift her that easily.

He settled her, and then put a curled finger under her chin. "Are you okay?"

She nodded. Her body was aflame and desire was a hot lick in her belly, but she was okay.

Ugh, maybe she was going into heat? This had to stop. She couldn't let this warrior distract her. Anything between them would only be temporary. He'd lose interest, and leave her with a battered, bleeding heart.

"Stay here while we get this sorted," he said.

Finley managed a nod.

She sat there and watched him work with security. He was incredibly competent, and she suddenly felt bad about calling him Commander Brawn. It was clear he was intelligent and experienced, and good at his job.

Another part of her hated that he and Captain Rodriguez looked so good standing beside each other. Rodriguez's dark-brown hair was in a tight ponytail, and she was in good shape. She'd have no trouble keeping up with Sabin. Finley's stomach clenched into unpleasant knots.

There was movement at the door, and Admiral Barber strode in. She was in her Space Corps uniform, but her eyes were still puffy from sleep. Several officers and Dr. Kemp were with her.

Finley shivered, suddenly feeling cold. The hard reality of almost losing her life was settling on her like a freezing cloud.

Dark memories stirred. The horrible helplessness and fear of being a captive, being locked in a damn hole in the ground, rose up like a choking hand. She reached for her elastic band and snapped it.

Breathe. You're safe.

"What is going on?" The admiral spotted the Kantos' body and her mouth flattened.

Sabin appeared, draping a blanket he'd found from who-knew-where over Finley's shoulders.

The captain and Sabin brought the admiral up to speed. At that moment, the paramedics and the cleanup crew arrived.

Finley reluctantly submitted to some poking and prodding from a young paramedic who looked like he should still be in high school. She watched a team in hazmat suits bag the alien body. Green smears remained on the floor, and she shuddered.

"You're lucky," the young paramedic said. "Your wounds are healing nicely. Now that we're allies with the Eon, I hope we can get our hands on some of that *havv*." The man took the monitoring patch off her. "And perhaps our hands on some Eon warriors." The man winked at her.

Finley didn't respond.

"Your vitals are fine, although your heart rate's a little fast. Understandable, considering."

Yes, mostly because Sabin was in the room.

As if he knew she was thinking of him, Sabin glanced over, his gaze zeroing directly on her. Thank God the monitoring patch was off or it would be going crazy.

The paramedic closed his case and patted her shoulder.

Sabin, the admiral, and Dr. Kemp came over to her.

"She's fine," the paramedic informed them.

"I'm very glad you weren't hurt," Admiral Barber said. "And that Security Commander Solann-Ath intervened."

"Dr. Delgado helped." Sabin gave her a small smile. "She hit the Kantos assassin over the head with some equipment. She probably saved my life."

Finley doubted he'd needed her help, but found herself smiling back. Then his words registered. "Assassin?"

His face turned serious. "That was a Kantos assassin, and the bug I killed in my quarters was its stalker, a hunting bug."

"So, the Kantos targeted you and Dr. Delgado." The admiral didn't look happy.

"It targeted Finley." Sabin scowled. "The bug was just keeping me busy."

Finley's gaze ran over her ruined model, where it lay trampled on the floor. "They know about the StarStorm, and want to stop it."

Sabin nodded.

Admiral Barber muttered a very un-admiral-like curse.

"We need to be very careful until we know how this assassin got on the planet, and what its exact plans were," Sabin said.

Captain Rodriguez's face darkened. "A single Kantos or a small team could easily get on planet. We don't have the same technology the Eon do. We'll pick up a large ship, but not a handful of Kantos trying to be stealthy."

And Finley assumed assassins were pretty stealthy.

"You think they'll try again?" the admiral asked.

Finley's pulse did a crazy little spike. *Great.* Was she now a main target of the Kantos?

"Right now, I'm not ruling anything out," Sabin said.

"We have to increase security." Barber frowned. "And Dr. Delgado needs protection."

"She has it," Sabin said. "Me."

Finley sucked in a breath.

"From now on—" his gaze collided with hers "—I'm with you every minute of the day."

SABIN ESCORTED Finley back to her quarters. She opened the door and he looked around. It had a similar layout to his, but in reverse. A few personal items were scattered around.

And it smelled like her.

He dragged in a breath and pulled the tantalizing scent deep into his senses. Sweet and spicy.

"Do you wear a scent?" he asked.

"What?" She'd been subdued as they left the lab, no doubt dealing with the aftermath of the attack.

"A scent? Perfume?"

Her brows creased. "No. But I shower with a hand-made soap. My mother makes it for me."

Sabin closed the door, not letting thoughts of Finley in the shower into his head. He dropped his bag of gear that he'd picked up from his quarters on the floor. "You've been quiet."

She walked into the living area. Her lab coat was

gone, taken by the containment team. She wrapped her arms around herself.

"Well, it's not every day a woman gets attacked by an alien assassin."

Sabin strode to her and gripped her shoulders. "I won't let them hurt you, Finley."

"I know. You want this weapons system up and running, too."

He let his hand slide up to cradle her face. They both knew it wasn't just that.

Her hands slid around his wrists, her eyes glowing. "Sabin..."

No. He couldn't risk losing control. He stepped back.

Her hands fell to her sides.

"Finley, what happened in the lab...it can't happen again."

She blinked. "The Kantos attack?"

"No, what happened after that."

"Me kissing you." Her chin lifted. "Although it should be noted that you kissed me back."

He balled his hands to stop from reaching for her. He saw a flash of uncertainty in her eyes.

"I shouldn't, but I'd like to do it again," she said softly.

"No." He shook his head. "It's not happening again. I cannot split my focus, especially for something as frivolous as an ill-advised attraction."

"Oh." The color leached from her cheeks. "I thought the kiss was... Well, I guess you didn't feel what I did."

Sabin's chest tightened and he watched her stand straighter, her hands clutching the hem of her shirt.

"You're right," she said. "We need to be sensible. I

have to get this weapons system complete. Especially since if I'm not focused, it might get me killed."

She was talking sense, but he still didn't like it. He hated seeing the uncertainty on her face. He wanted to reach for her and...

Her stomach growled.

"You missed the dinner tonight." He'd definitely noticed that she was conspicuously absent from the meal. "What did you eat?"

She pressed a hand to her belly. "Um, I don't think I ate anything." Her cheeks flushed. "Well, just a few marshmallows from my secret stash." She shrugged a shoulder. "I sometimes forget to eat when I'm busy with my work."

He frowned. He didn't like that. "Come on." He led her to her kitchen and opened the cooling unit—what was it called, again? Oh, yes. The refrigerator.

And instantly realized he didn't know what anything was.

Shaking her head, she nudged him aside. She pulled out a block of something yellow. And some sort of fruit—small, red, ball-shaped objects. From the cupboard beside the fridge, she pulled out some small, flat circles.

They sat at the table and she cut bits from the yellow block and put it on a circle.

She eyed him. "Cheese and crackers." She held one out to him. "I'm guessing Earth food won't kill you?"

"It's highly unlikely. My helian would detect the presence of anything that didn't agree with my Eon physiology." He gingerly took the cracker and took a bite. Interesting flavors hit his senses.

"More?" she asked

He nodded.

They ate quietly together.

"Here. Try a grape." She passed over one of the red balls.

Sweetness burst over his tongue.

"You like them?" she said with a smile.

"They're delicious."

Her lips tilted into a smile, and she rose and went back into the kitchen.

"Here."

There were more small, red fruits. Some dark squares, and a round, soft wheel of something.

"Raspberries. Dark chocolate. And another type of cheese called brie."

She fed him small bits, and each different taste exploded in Sabin's mouth. He groaned.

He opened his eyes to find her staring at his mouth.

"Finley..."

Sabin wasn't sure if he moved or she did, but they were kissing again. Her hand slid into his hair and he stroked her tongue with his. She tasted better than any Terran delicacy.

He could drown in the tastes of her, and never get enough.

No.

"Cren." He yanked back, then jerked to his feet. "*No.* We're not doing this."

"Sabin." She blinked, her brow creased. "What are you so afraid of?"

"That this—" he waved a hand between them "—will

take over. That I won't focus on our work, and that I'll fail people."

He couldn't spell out just how dangerous it would be for him to lose his control. The way she teased all his senses was deadly.

"Right." She nodded. "I have an entire planet to protect. That's what I need to focus on. I can't let more people die." Her voice cracked.

"It's not your sole responsibility. You're not alone."

"I'm always alone." She shook her head again. "Sorry, I won't kiss you again. I seem to be attracted to big, athletic, muscular men. It's like my kryptonite."

Sabin had no idea what kryptonite was, but he made a note to look it up. "Finley."

"I'll respect your wishes to not cross any personal lines, Security Commander Solann-Ath."

The way she said his name was like a whip to his skin. Sabin could almost see the wall she was building between them.

"You're right that this attraction is a waste of time," she said. "There are other more important things to focus on."

Sabin's body was stiff. *A waste of time.* He'd heard his parents use the same terms to describe his uncle and his indulgences. "Yes. This attraction wouldn't last long anyway. And our work should be our only priority." He schooled his features to show no emotion.

Finley looked like he'd hit her, then swallowed. "Right."

"Get some sleep, Finley. It's been a long day. Tomorrow, we'll turn all our attention to the project. The sooner the StarStorm is operational, the sooner the Kantos will stop targeting you and your planet."

"Right." She clasped her hands together.

"And the sooner I'll leave."

Something flashed in her eyes. "Got it." Her voice was a whisper.

"Go to bed, Finley. And don't worry, I'll sleep on the couch and ensure you aren't in any danger."

She looked like she wanted to say something, but she just nodded. "Good night, Sabin."

She turned and went to her bedroom. The door closed with a definite click.

Sabin blew out a breath, her scent still teasing him.

His control right now was a shaky thing. He wanted to lunge after her. His helian pulsed, and he fought back his emotions.

He'd protect her, help her with her work, and that was it.

He couldn't risk anything else.

CHAPTER FIVE

D*arkness. Crying. Screaming. Fear.*
      Thick, choking, never-ending fear.

With a sob, Finley shoved at the bindings holding her. She had to help Brent and Melody. She had to find a way to escape.

She sat up, her heart pounding as she searched for her captors, waiting for a blow to come. Waiting to hear Melody's sobs or Brent's moans of pain.

Silvery darkness greeted her and she realized her bindings were her twisted, sweat-dampened sheets. Moonlight streamed through the gaps in her blinds.

She pressed a shaky hand to her forehead. *Nightmare.* She hadn't had one for over a year. The Kantos attack must have triggered it. She reached for her elastic and snapped it hard, welcoming the sting that kept her grounded.

Her bedroom door slammed open and a big, broad shape loomed.

Finley blinked, taking in Sabin's near-naked form. He

wore a pair of snug, black boxers that left little to the imagination.

And her lust-riddled brain was more than happy to imagine all kinds of things.

Remember the warrior had made it very clear he isn't interested in you.

Sabin scanned the room, hands raised, then his gaze zeroed in on her. His gaze dropped to where she toyed with the band.

"Are you all right?" he asked.

"Fine." She jerked the sheet up to cover her tiny tank top and shorts.

"What woke you?"

"Nothing."

"Finley."

She huffed out a breath. "There are no Kantos, warrior. You can go."

He didn't budge.

Stubborn man. She sighed. "You aren't going to leave, are you?"

"No."

"I had a nightmare."

Even in the dim moonlight, she saw his scowl deepen. "About the attack?"

"No. I think that just triggered it." She pushed her tangled hair back, pulling in some calming breaths. "I'm fine. Go back to sleep."

Instead, he moved closer.

Finley stiffened.

"What was your nightmare about?"

"I don't remember," she clipped out.

He sat on the side of her bed. "Would you like to talk about it?"

"No." Nope. Definitely not.

He was silent and she plucked at her sheet. She could feel him looking at her.

"There's nothing you can do," she said quietly. "Some old scars never go away."

"Yes, I know."

The deep edge to his voice made her look up. *What scars did he have?* He looked so strong, so handsome and perfect.

"But you face them, accept them, and do your best not to let them cripple you." He said the words matter-of-factly.

"I hate being afraid," she whispered.

He reached out and grabbed her hand. "You face that too." He squeezed her fingers. "You aren't alone."

Her throat tight, she held his hand and nodded.

"The band...it helps you?" he asked.

She nodded.

"Will you be able to get back to sleep?"

She shrugged. Often after a bad dream, she lay awake the rest of the night, not wanting to risk another terror-drenched nightmare.

"What helps?" he asked.

Funnily enough, not being alone helped. He'd already given her that. "Sometimes, I like to listen to music."

"Then put some music on."

She hesitated, then let him go and leaned across to

the small comp unit beside her bed. She touched the buttons and her favorite indie band came on.

A woman's throaty, haunting voice filled the room.

Sabin paused and his head tilted. "I like this."

She watched him close his eyes, looking like he was losing himself in the music. She'd had a picture of Eon warriors as boring, stoic, military types. But watching the way Sabin moved, ate, and listened to the music, it was like he appreciated every new sensation.

Finley lay back on her pillows. The singer's voice changed the tense atmosphere to something relaxed and hushed.

"Sleep now, Finley," Sabin said.

Her eyelids fluttered, tiredness pulling on her. Knowing he was sitting there, sharing the darkness with her, made her feel safe.

It didn't matter that he didn't want her like she wanted him. It didn't matter that he was an alien warrior assigned to protect her. He was here and she liked it way too much.

A second later, sleep pulled her under.

SABIN STOOD at the welcome lunch for the warriors, arms crossed over his chest.

"How many welcome gatherings are there going to be?" Rade grumbled.

"The Terrans are just trying to do their bit to show their dedication to the alliance," Sabin said.

"I'd prefer to be working," Gadon said.

"Me, too." Sabin's gaze went to Finley.

Unsurprisingly, she was at the opposite end of the room to him.

This morning in the lab, there'd been an awkward tension combined with the simmering attraction between them.

Sabin couldn't shake the feeling he'd hurt her.

His hand clenched. He *had* to get this desire under control.

"Do you think the Kantos will attack your scientist again?" Rade asked.

"I'm not going to let her get hurt. I sent my report to my war commander. They're compiling all intel they have on the Kantos assassins."

The Kantos wouldn't get another chance to hurt Finley. Or inspire more nightmares for her.

"Drink?" A smiling woman with dark hair and bright-blue eyes materialized in front of Sabin. She held out a glass of something clear and fizzy.

"Be nice," Gadon whispered. "Your scowl is scaring people."

Sabin managed a smile. "Thank you." He sniffed the drink. It was water with the scent of citrus.

"I'm Whitney." A cloud of strong scent wafted over him. She was wearing a very intense perfume that smelled like a garden of flowers.

"You're a scientist?" he asked.

She moved closer, her arm brushing his. The scent intensified—cloying musk and flowers. It wasn't to his taste.

"No. I'm an administrator. I keep all these geeks organized. They'd forget to eat or sleep, otherwise."

That just reminded him of the late-night meal he'd shared with Finley. The small tastes, the kiss.

His helian pulsed, and he shifted. Whitney pressed a hand to his arm and leaned in, her breast brushing him.

"Are you enjoying Earth?" she asked.

"It appears to be a nice planet, but I'm here to work."

She stroked his arm. "Surely you get some time off. I could show you around."

Her scent nearly overpowered his senses and he felt the need to get away. Did she not understand the severity of the Kantos? Her entire planet was at stake.

He lifted his head.

Finley was watching them. Her gaze hit his, dropped to Whitney, then skated away. She turned her back to him.

"No, I don't have time off."

Whitney's lips—painted a very shiny pink—tipped down. "What about in the evenings?" Her voice was almost a low purr. "Have you ever been with a Terran woman? You're so big. I bet we'd have a good time."

Sabin felt nothing. No heat, no lick of desire. "I'm currently assigned to protect Dr. Delgado."

Whitney's nose wrinkled. "Devil Delgado. I'm so sorry you've been saddled with her."

Finley stiffened and Sabin knew she'd heard Whitney's words. He watched as Finley murmured something to the people beside her, then moved across the room.

Cren. He tensed. He'd warned her not to go

anywhere without him. "Dr. Delgado is a brilliant scientist. I'm honored to protect her."

"Oh." Sensing something in his hard tone, Whitney looked uncomfortable.

Sabin saw Finley pause at the restrooms and slip inside.

Whitney eyed Rade and the warrior lifted his drink, clearly not wanting to be Whitney's next target.

Sabin frowned at the restroom door, waiting for Finley to return.

His communicator pinged. He pulled it out and saw a call from Malax.

"Excuse me." He stepped away from Whitney. "Malax."

His war commander looked grim. "Sabin."

Sabin's hand clenched on the communicator. "What?"

"We received intel on the Kantos assassins from Davion on the *Desteron*." War Commander Davion Thann-Eon was the first warrior to mate with a Terran, after Eve Traynor had abducted him.

"It appears the assassins work in a small pack. Usually, three or four assassins and their stalkers."

Sabin swallowed a curse. "So, there are likely more here."

"Yes. They're bred for stealth, very good at avoiding detection, and very focused on their target."

Which meant they'd try to attack Finley again.

"Sabin?" Rade moved closer.

Gadon was right behind him, frowning.

"The Kantos sent a team of the assassins after Finley," Sabin told them.

The other warriors scowled.

"Sabin, keep her safe, and get the StarStorm operational," Malax said. "Fast."

"Yes, War Commander."

"Security Commander?" Admiral Barber appeared, Captain Rodriguez behind her. "Is there a problem?"

"My war commander just confirmed that the Kantos didn't send just one assassin, they sent a team of assassins after Finley."

The admiral gasped and Captain Rodriguez cursed.

Sabin looked at the bathroom door again. Finley had been gone a long time.

He felt a prickle along his senses. He strode across the room.

"Security Commander!" the Admiral called.

He reached the door. Whitney was standing nearby with some other women.

"That's the ladies'," Whitney said. "You can't go in there."

He shoved the door open.

The tiled room was empty.

The window was blown out, just ragged shards of glass left behind.

There was no sign of Finley.

"Rade! Gadon!" he bellowed.

Then, heedless of the fact that he was two stories up, Sabin leaped out the window.

FINLEY STOMPED INTO THE BATHROOM, her belly churning.

Ugh. She pressed her hands to the edge of the sink. She was a mess. She was angry, jealous, hurt.

See, this was why she steered clear of men.

Last night, Sabin had just switched off. It was clear that despite the attraction between them, he didn't want her enough. He'd turned it off like it didn't matter. Like she was so easily ignored and shunted aside.

Every other man had easily ignored her, so she shouldn't be surprised.

Yet, he'd comforted her after her nightmare and stayed with her until she'd fallen asleep.

She looked in the mirror. An ugly twist of emotions tightened in her chest. She barely knew the man. Hell, she'd agreed they should keep things professional.

But her body didn't agree.

Then he let pretty, pouty Whitney crawl all over him.

Finley blew out a breath. Okay, maybe not crawl over him, exactly, but there was definite flirting going on. He'd smiled at her.

"Oh, your muscles are so big." Finley rolled her eyes. Then she caught her gaze in the mirror.

She wanted him. She wanted Sabin's big arms around her. After her nightmare, she'd dreamed about him the rest of the night.

"Goddammit." She was all messed up. There was a hot ball of hurt and jealousy in her chest, and she clearly wasn't focused on her project. "Get yourself together, Finley."

She raised her head.

And met the multi-eyed gaze of a Kantos assassin right behind her.

Finley's adrenaline spiked, and she opened her mouth to scream.

The alien lunged.

It wrapped his arms and wings around her, and all she could see was black.

A clawed hand slammed over her mouth. She jerked and bit it. Oh, yuck, she was biting an insectoid alien.

The alien made a sound and spun toward the window. Its wings shifted enough for her to see the grassy area, two stories down.

Oh, no.

It lifted its other hand, and she saw that it was holding a small device.

Suddenly, the window shattered soundlessly, glass falling like it had been put on mute.

The device was somehow canceling the sound.

She fought and twisted, but the creature's wings were holding her too tight.

Then the alien jumped out the window.

Finley screamed against the assassin's palm. Its wings snapped out and their drop slowed, and they hit the ground without crashing.

She went crazy. She twisted, jerked, kicked. If the Kantos dragged her away, she was as good as dead.

They fell and hit the grass. *Where the hell was everyone?*

She kicked again, catching something with the heel of

her shoe, and the wings loosened. Finley broke free, leaped up, and ran.

Behind her, she heard a screech and a flap of wings. She looked back over her shoulder.

Dread filled her like concrete.

The Kantos was in the air, a few feet off the ground, wings spread. It looked like a demon from Hell.

Her heart lodged firmly in her throat.

The Kantos shot downward.

Finley dove and rolled across the grass.

The assassin landed and advanced.

She tried to scramble away. It swung its claws toward her.

A piercing pain in her shoulder. She screamed. It was as though burning knives had sliced into her.

The beast had rammed its claws through her skin and muscle. *Shit, shit, shit.* She suddenly realized that it was worse than that—the alien's claws had gone through her shoulder, into the grass and dirt below, pinning her there.

The assassin opened its mouth, and that ugly protuberance extended.

So gross. She turned her head and tried to move, but the pain from the claws embedded in her almost made her black out.

Then, a deep roar filled the air.

Sabin crashed into the Kantos, tackling it off her.

The claws pulled free and she swallowed a scream, pain sending black spots dancing in front of her eyes.

Her heart was pounding like a drum, and she slapped a hand over her bleeding shoulder. She managed to struggle into a sitting position.

Sabin once again wore his black-scale armor, and had a long sword on one arm.

He and the Kantos rolled, then Sabin rose on one knee. His sword raked across the Kantos' chest.

With a deafening screech, the alien rushed at Sabin, claws slashing.

The pair moved so fast that they were a blur of sword and claws.

The pounding sound of running footsteps caught her ears. The other two warriors, also in scale armor, appeared, their swords lifted. They watched Sabin and the Kantos like hawks.

One glanced at her. "Are you all right, Dr. Delgado?"

"Yes. Just help Sabin."

The Kantos assassin took to the air, hovering.

Sabin rose, bent his knees, and leaped into the air incredibly high. He lifted his sword above his head and brought it down.

The Kantos dodged, but the sword clipped its wing.

With a wild screech, it crashed to the ground.

All of a sudden, with a wild growl, a dog-sized creature flew out of the bushes. Its back was covered in spikes. It aimed right at Sabin.

Oh God, another Kantos bug. It leaped onto Sabin's back.

The assassin spun and ran.

"Don't let it escape," Sabin roared.

The two warriors spun and chased after the assassin.

Sabin whirled, trying to get the bug off his back.

She had to help him.

Ignoring the blood oozing from her shoulder, she

looked around. She grabbed a stick off the grass, and leaped forward.

Finley swung it and whacked the bug's head. She swung again, hitting its quivering antennae.

The bug released Sabin, landed on the grass, and spun to face Finley.

Uh-oh. The spikes along its back quivered, its mandibles opening and closing menacingly.

She backed up, gripping the stick hard.

Then a sword slashed down, cutting the bug's head clean off its body. Green blood sprayed on the grass and sizzled where it landed.

Oh, God.

Finley's legs collapsed, and she hit the ground on her butt.

"Finley."

Sabin dropped down beside her and wrapped his arms around her. He was big, strong, solid. And he'd just saved her...again.

She burrowed into his chest and held on tight, burying her face in his neck.

"*Cren.* Finley." She felt his chest shudder.

She stared at his shoulder, and the scratches through his armor, revealing his skin. "You're hurt."

"It's already healing. My helian will slow the blood loss and increase cellular repair."

Wow. That must be nice. She could do with some of that, right now.

He pulled back, a fierce look in his eyes. "You're hurt, too."

Despite the look on his face, his hands were gentle. He touched her shoulder wound.

She winced, dizziness crowding her head. "Um, Sabin?"

"Yes?"

"I'm pretty sure I'm about to pass out." Her vision swirled, and then everything went black.

CHAPTER SIX

An unfamiliar sensation sat low in Sabin's chest. He held Finley tighter, and realized that the slick, oily sensation was fear.

The urge to kill the Kantos again, to pummel it into oblivion rose up. It took all his control to wrestle the need into submission.

Finley needed him.

He saw the ugly wound on her shoulder, smelled the iron-rich scent of her blood. Her eyelashes fluttered as she regained consciousness. *Thank the warriors.* Her heartbeat was strong.

"You're okay. You're safe."

She licked her lips. "It wasn't just a bad dream?" She eyed the dead bug and grimaced.

"I am afraid not. Don't worry. I've got you."

Space Corps Security swarmed around them, a containment team sliding the bug into a bag. Another man started to burn the grassy area with a flamethrower.

Rade and Gadon reappeared, Rade dragging the

dead assassin behind him. Both warriors were splattered with Kantos blood and gore.

Finley whimpered, and Sabin rose with her in his arms. She held on tight.

"Security Commander, the paramedics are on the way." Captain Rodriguez eyed Finley's injury. "She might need the hospital, and surgery."

"No, I can care for her. My *havv* will heal her faster and better."

Rodriguez looked like she wanted to argue.

"Sabin, we need to discuss this." Admiral Barber strode forward, her hands clasped behind her back. "We need to make a plan to ensure Dr. Delgado's safety, and still get the StarStorm completed."

Sabin nodded. "Later. When she's recovered and had a chance to rest."

He strode across the grass to the research building. Moments later, he set her down on the couch in her quarters.

"How are you doing?" Her face was still white.

"It hurts." Lines of pain bracketed her mouth.

Sabin sat down beside her and started to undo the buttons of her shirt. She grabbed his hands.

"Let me take care of you," he murmured.

He felt a driving need to look after her. To heal her, comfort her. He couldn't seem to keep his distance from this woman. How had she turned his life upside down so quickly?

She swallowed. "Wouldn't you prefer to be with Whitney?"

He frowned. "Who?"

Finley made an annoyed sound. "The woman you were flirting with at lunch."

"Oh, Whitney." He stilled. Finley was jealous. A part of him liked that.

He spread her shirt open, then commanded his helian to form a small knife.

Finley gasped. He cut her shirt off, leaving her in a froth of pale-green lace. It cupped her generous breasts.

"I like the pretty things you wear under your sensible clothes."

"I'm...I'm not considered beautiful here. Whitney is. Slim, perfect features..."

He touched Finley's shoulder. "I like strength with some softness. I like my bed partners not to be tiny like children."

"Oh."

As he studied the wound, his jaw tightened. "I promised that I wouldn't let the Kantos hurt you again."

"I'm okay, Sabin. I'm alive thanks to you."

He took out some *havv* and squeezed the liquid onto her wound. She bit her lip. "It burns."

"The more significant the wound, the more it hurts." He held her hand and tangled their fingers together.

Seeing that assassin on her...

Sabin fought back a rush of feelings.

Finley cocked her head. "I can feel your mood."

"My helian amplifies my emotions."

"What are you feeling?"

"Guilt, residual fear."

Her lips parted.

"Relief." He stroked her fingers, her palm. "Desire."

"Sabin." Her voice was breathy.

"You need to eat or drink something. Healing requires energy." He rose. She was hurt, and he needed to take care of her, not think about getting her naked.

"I have some protein packets in the cupboard," she said. "You just mix them with milk." She leaned back on the pillows on the couch. "I have them when I don't want to cook." She sent him a small smile. "Which is a lot."

He found the packets and mixed one in a glass with the liquid labeled milk. He sniffed the milk. "What is this?"

"It comes from an animal called a cow."

He stilled. "A real, live animal?"

"Yes."

He shuddered and brought the drink back to her. She sipped it.

"All of it." He pushed the glass back to her mouth.

"I've been taking care of myself for a long time, Sabin."

"Not today." He set the empty glass down on the coffee table. "I'm sorry the assassin got to you. I should have—"

Finley pressed a hand to his chest. "You *saved* me. I knew you'd come. I'm glad Whitney didn't keep you distracted for too long."

"I'm not interested in Whitney. I'm sure she's very nice, just very...forward. And she wears too much scent."

He stroked Finley's arm and could already see that her wound was slowly healing. He stroked the unmarked skin beside it, and she shivered.

"I prefer the subtle scent of spicy sweetness. And smooth, golden skin."

Finley bit her lip. "I'm not sure this is keeping things professional."

"It's not, but I can't seem to remain professional around you, Finley."

She sucked in a breath. "Really?"

"Really." He needed to touch her. Needed the feel of her skin as reassurance that she was all right. "I can't seem to stop how I feel."

He ran his hand down her arm, soaking in the feel of her. Her skin was so smooth. He lifted her hand, and pressed his lips to her wrist, then her elbow.

She pulled in a sharp breath.

He let his other hand brush her collarbone and he scented her arousal.

"I never imagined Eon warriors would be so...sensual," she said.

"We're men as well as warriors, but I am a special case."

"Oh?"

Sabin hesitated. "I have extra-enhanced senses."

"Really?"

"Yes. I feel more, smell more." He couldn't control the edge in his voice.

Her mouth opened. "It causes you problems?"

"It can. That's why I maintain rigid control." Sabin allowed himself to indulge his senses a little, but he wouldn't risk hurting her. It was a dangerous line to walk.

He checked her wound again. "It's knitting well."

"Good."

He lowered his mouth, kissed her healing marks.

"Oh, God." A soft expulsion of air.

"We take things one day at a time, Finley," he said. "For now, you rest and heal. Tomorrow, we'll talk about further steps to keep you safe." He tucked her hair behind her ear. "You're my only priority."

FINLEY LOOKED in the bathroom mirror the next morning. She was still in her pajama boxer shorts and a tank top. She pulled the top's neckline down and prodded the site of her wound.

It was gone. There was a faint pinkness to the newly healed skin, but that was it.

Amazing.

She swallowed. It was far too easy to think of the attack. The assassin hunting her. She closed her eyes and took a few deep breaths.

She was safe. Sabin was literally one room away.

Her belly clenched.

How the hell was she supposed to focus on her work, when they were going to be glued together? How was she going to keep her hormones in check?

And he'd admitted that he felt the same, but that he needed to stay in control.

She could do this.

She was a professional. She had to focus on the project.

Setting her shoulders back, she dredged up some self-control. She was a smart, sensible woman.

Spinning, she yanked open the door and ran into a very hard, very bare chest.

Finley's mouth went dry. She blinked rapidly.

Sabin stood before her, clad only in black shorts, his wide chest covered in bronze skin.

She swallowed. *Wow.* Carved muscles. Hard pecs. Ridges and dips down his abs. Desire pulsed between her legs.

"Good morning." His voice still held the deep, growly edge of sleep.

"Hi." God, her voice was a squeak. "Did you sleep well?"

He nodded, but she couldn't drag her gaze off his chest. Her pulse was doing a crazy dance.

"Finley?"

She managed to jerk her gaze up. He was smiling. "The admiral called. We have a meeting in her office in thirty minutes."

Finley gasped. "I need breakfast, then a shower."

"I'll let you sort out breakfast, and I'll wash up first."

"Right." She usually had cereal, but she guessed with his muscle mass he'd need some protein.

He brushed past her—all that hot, hard male. She stifled a whimper.

Get it together, Finley.

She made eggs. Sabin wolfed them down, so he clearly liked them. She showered quickly and put on her usual work clothes—black pants and a white shirt.

Soon, they headed to the admiral's office. Two young, uniformed Space Corps cadets waved them through.

Admiral Barber stood at the window, her uniform

neatly pressed, her ash-blonde hair ruthlessly styled. Captain Rodriguez sat in a nearby chair, her long legs crossed. Beside her, sat Dr. Kemp.

"Security Commander, Dr. Delgado, please take a seat," the admiral said.

Sabin pulled a chair out for Finley and she sat. He stood behind her, a comforting presence.

"Security Commander, if you could update us."

Sabin nodded and pulled out a tablet-like device. "We've confirmed the Kantos assassins are normally sent in a group. There are likely still one or two more on the planet."

Finley's stomach churned.

"I've increased security patrols around headquarters," Rodriguez said.

"It won't be enough," Sabin said. "The Kantos won't stop. They'll keep coming after Finley. They want to stop the StarStorm."

The damn Kantos were like a plague of locusts. They'd just keep sending more assassins. Finley clenched her hands together.

"Finley needs to be moved to a secure location," Sabin said.

Her stomach dropped away. They wanted to treat her like a prisoner? "No." She didn't want to be locked up. "My work, my lab—"

"There must be other labs where she can work. And where we can keep the location secret."

"But I'm almost at the testing stage."

The admiral steepled her hands together on her desk. "It's a good idea."

"Admiral." Finley swallowed. "I can't leave my project. I need my lab and equipment." Her voice cracked. "I can't be locked up with no light or air."

Sympathy crossed the Admiral's face. "It won't come to that."

Sabin frowned, gaze swinging between them. "What's going on?"

Finley didn't want him to know. She tried to form some words.

"Six years ago, Dr. Delgado and two colleagues were abducted by terrorists. They were kept in captivity for a week."

Finley squeezed her eyes closed and tried not to let the memories rush back in. She felt a dark throb of emotion from Sabin.

"She was rescued by a special-forces team a week later," Admiral Barber continued. "Unfortunately, her colleagues didn't make it."

Finley opened her eyes. "Their names were Brent and Melody."

The admiral inclined her head. Big hands came down on Finley's shoulders, squeezed. Instantly, she felt safe and reassured.

"I will not let anyone lock you away, Finley," Sabin promised quietly.

"We can find you a secure lab somewhere secret. Some place where you can get outside, but also safely continue your work." The admiral looked at Sabin. "You'll be in charge of her security."

He nodded.

Finley felt a strange mix of emotions. Just her and

Sabin locked in a lab together in the middle of nowhere. She was honest enough to admit that she liked the idea.

"I have a place in mind." Barber sat back in her chair. "No one outside of this room will have your location. Dr. Delgado, you'll leave today. It is the highest priority that you and the Security Commander complete the Star-Storm system."

Finley nodded.

"You won't be able to contact your family. I'll ensure that they know you're safe."

Oh, her parents wouldn't like that very much.

"Where is the lab?" Sabin asked.

"It's extremely remote. It's located in a military base in the center of the Australian desert."

Finley raised her brows. "Australia?"

Barber nodded. "The Woomera Range Complex."

Finley blew out a breath. She knew about the weapons complex. It'd been used for weapons testing for years, and would likely have very good facilities for her.

Not to mention being very remote, and hours and hours from any cities.

"I suggest the other warriors stay here at headquarters," the admiral said. "If all of you disappear, I think it would attract too much attention."

"Agreed," Sabin said.

"So, pack and change. A helicopter will take you to the airport, Ellington Field. From there, a private jet will take you to Australia."

Finley drew in a breath. "Okay. I need some equipment from my lab."

The admiral nodded. "Do it. I'll arrange a team to

pack it up and ship it. Good luck to both of you. The fate of our planet and its people are in your hands."

Finley swallowed. *No pressure.* She shook hands with the admiral, then she and Sabin headed into the hall.

"Are you all right?" he asked.

"Fine." Finley liked routine and structure. This was a big upheaval.

Well, Finley, you can be inconvenienced but alive, or dead. If she stayed here, she'd put other people at risk as well.

Sabin stopped, and pressed a finger under her chin. "I am sorry to hear about your abduction. It must have been a terrible ordeal."

"More terrible for my friends that died."

"That was the cause of your nightmare."

She nodded.

"I'm glad you survived, Finley."

Not a day went by where she didn't feel guilty about it.

"Everything will be okay," Sabin said.

The strength in his voice made her want to believe it. She nodded.

"I'll be with you every step of the way."

CHAPTER SEVEN

S abin glanced over at Finley. She'd worked most of the flight with a computer and tablet open. Even now, she was hunched over her laptop, her fingers tapping and her brow creased in concentration. A forgotten mug of the drink she called coffee sat at her elbow.

He felt a tightness in his chest. He just wanted to get to their destination and get her safe. He didn't like being in the air in an aircraft that wasn't equipped with any weapons. He'd been on edge the entire flight.

He looked out the window. Below them lay a desolate, orange-red landscape. They appeared to be in a very isolated part of the Earth.

One of the pilots strode out of the cockpit. "We'll be landing soon."

"Great." Finley stretched her neck side to side.

"Where are we exactly?" Sabin asked.

"The southern part of the country of Australia. It's an island continent in the southern hemisphere, and very remote. We're almost at the Woomera Range Complex. It's a base run by the Australian Air Force. It has the lab and testing facilities you need, Dr. Delgado."

"And security?" Sabin asked.

The pilot nodded. "Its biggest defense is its isolation, but it also has top-of-the-line security systems, and a well-trained security team."

Sabin wouldn't relax until he'd assessed it himself.

Soon, the plane started its descent. Finley packed up her gear, fidgeting in her seat. He put his hand over hers.

"It's going to be fine."

She gave a short nod. "I'm just eager to see the lab, and get back to work."

He stroked her fingers and saw her small shudder.

"Don't tease me," she whispered.

He made a humming noise. "I can't seem to stop."

"Sabin, I'm on the edge here." She breathed deep. "I don't play games. I want you. Badly. You keep up the small touches and I'll throw myself at you."

His gut tightened. The thought of her in his arms...

Cren, he needed some control. What if he lost it with her, hurt her?

"Sabin?" Her fingers wrapped around his.

"I don't want to hurt you."

"What do you mean?"

"My extra-sensory issues..." He dragged in a breath. He hated exposing any weakness. "I had an uncle who had the same condition. He lost control. Indulged all of his senses and desires."

She bit her lip. "And?"

"He had a mate. He hurt her." In so many different ways.

Finley was silent a moment. "I haven't known you long, Sabin, but I don't think you'd ever hurt a woman."

"My uncle brought shame to my family. He was weak."

"It sounded like he needed help. Was he a warrior?"

Sabin shook his head.

"So, he didn't have your training or control?"

"Irrelevant. I won't risk hurting you."

They landed, the plane pulling up at a large hangar. Sabin studied the sprawl of buildings. The admiral had told him that a large percentage of the base was underground—for security, and to keep it protected from the harsh weather.

The rest of their surroundings consisted of orange-red dirt, rocks, and a few hardy, spindly bushes. He liked the harsh landscape.

They descended the stairs of the plane and found three people waiting for them.

"Dr. Delgado, Security Commander Solann-Ath." An older woman with white hair stepped forward. The woman looked friendly, like a favorite grandmother, but she had eyes that reflected her experience. "I'm Dr. Amelia Gregson, the head of the Woomera Range Complex. Welcome."

"Thank you." Finley shook the woman's hand.

Sabin followed suit.

"This is Dr. Ian Cho. He'll show you to your lab."

Dr. Cho was young, and wore thick glasses over his

dark eyes. His black hair flopped over his forehead, and he had a stain on his lab coat.

"It's a real pleasure." He pumped Finley's hand. "I'm a huge fan of your work, Dr. Delgado."

"That's great." She extricated her hand.

Dr. Cho looked at Sabin, hesitated, then offered a small wave. "Please, call me Ian. We don't stand on too much ceremony around here."

Dr. Gregson nodded at the final person. "And this is our head of security, Commander Kaira Chand."

Sabin took in the small woman and raised his brows. She was very short, but she did have a fit, compact body, and wore mottled, green-brown fatigues. Her dark-brown hair was pulled back, and she had dark eyes that were almost black, and brown skin.

"A pleasure." The woman nodded. "Security Commander, I'm guessing you'll want to assess base security." She had an authoritative, competent voice.

"I would," he replied.

"I'll be happy to show you around. And you know more about the Kantos threat than anyone. I'd like your thoughts and advice on any improvements we can make. My highest priority is to keep Dr. Delgado, and our base personnel, safe."

Sabin nodded. He added smart to Commander Kaira Chand's qualities. "Let's meet after I get Dr. Delgado settled."

"I'll let Dr. Cho and Commander Chand show you around." With a nod, Dr. Gregson left.

They walked inside, and cool air from the air conditioning hit his skin. The wide corridors were sparse, the decor simple. They passed a few scientists clad in casual clothes.

Ian Cho was like an excited pet, talking fast. The scientist led them down some stairs and into an elevator. They moved down several levels, and he led them down a corridor into a lab.

"This lab wasn't being used. We moved in some equipment we thought you'd need, and I believe yours arrives today on a cargo plane." The young man threw out an arm. "We'll get it set up for you straightaway."

Finley walked along the empty benches. It was underground so there were no windows. That made Sabin happy; fewer points of entry for the Kantos.

But it was also a concern. If assassins got in, Finley would be trapped.

"I'm so excited to work with you!" Ian said. "And another assistant, Dr. Gemma Neely, has been assigned to work with you to help you on your project. Gemma's awesome and super smart."

Finley spun. "I work alone."

"Ah." Ian looked awkward. "I was told that I had to assign you some people to help. That getting the Star-Storm operational was top priority."

Finley huffed out a breath. "Fine, but if you aren't up to par, you aren't staying."

Sabin spun to Kaira. "Are there any emergency exits?"

The security commander shook her head.

"We need to build a safe room. Somewhere Finley can lock herself in. Just in case."

He saw fear flash in Finley's brown eyes. He wanted

to comfort her, but instead curled his fingers into his palm.

Then she straightened. "Whatever we need to do."

He smiled at her. He loved her toughness.

"I'll organize it," Kaira said.

"The lab is adequate," Finley said. "I want to get started straight away."

The others left, and Sabin helped Finley set up her computers. Ian had left instructions on how to access Woomera's secure network. Sabin leaned against the bench, watching Finley work. He'd never watched someone work and enjoyed it before.

It didn't take long for her to get lost in her work. Occasionally, she muttered to herself. It was clear she thrived on the challenge. She liked solving problems.

He pulled out his own work and started going through the code for the targeting system. But he couldn't stop glancing her way.

She looked at him and blinked. "Why are you staring?"

"You're easy to stare at."

Her eyes flashed. "Come over here and take a look at this targeting information."

"So, you do want me for more than just my muscles?"

She stilled. "Sabin, I am sorry I called you Commander Brawn. It's clear that you're very good at your job."

"Hey." He rested his hands on her shoulders. "I was teasing."

"I'm sorry. It was rude." She shot him a rueful smile. "I'm told I can often be rude."

He ran a finger down her nose. "Luckily, I like it. I seem to like everything about you. Now, let's get to work."

FINLEY LOOKED up from her computer and blinked.

Her simulations were looking good, and she smiled. They might be ready to do a ground test soon. Sabin's input had really helped.

She looked around. The lab was empty. He'd gone to check on base security with Kaira Chand.

If the ground test worked, they could move to orbital tests.

"We'll be ready for you, you ugly bugs."

Finley arched her back. She'd kicked her shoes off at some stage and she looked around. She had no idea where they were. An empty packet of marshmallows sat on her desk. She didn't even remember eating them.

She glanced at her watch. *Crap.* It was nine o'clock at night. Without windows, it was easy to lose track of time.

Nearby was a tray that Ian had brought for her, with the dinner that she'd picked at. It was probably time to find her quarters, but she wasn't tired. Thanks to jetlag, she was feeling kind of wired.

She heard a noise in the hall and her heart jumped into her throat. She grabbed a wireless keyboard and lifted it. If it was another Kantos assassin, she wasn't going down without a fight.

She crept toward the door.

It started to swing open, and her pulse spiked. She swung the keyboard.

Sabin caught it with one hand.

"Oh, God," she cried, slumping.

He held the keyboard up. "You thought this would stop me?"

"I wasn't trying to stop *you*. I thought you were a Kantos assassin."

He arched a brow, then his fingers clenched. The keyboard crumpled.

She sniffed. "Show off."

"The Kantos would've knocked this aside like a twig."

She moved back into the lab. "You made your point."

"Do you have any combat training?"

She spun. "What? No, I'm a scientist, not a soldier."

"Basic self-defense is a good idea for anybody."

She chewed her lip. She'd taken some classes after her abduction, but she wasn't very coordinated, and had felt like an idiot. "Said the big alien warrior." She crossed her arms over her chest. "I'm not very athletic."

"I think we should add some self-defense lessons to your schedule. Just in case an assassin gets through."

She didn't have time for fighting lessons. She opened her mouth to argue—

"Or one manages to take me down."

Her mouth clicked shut and her mind went blank. *No.* She couldn't—and didn't want to imagine—Sabin going down.

God. She pressed a hand to her stomach. She thought about those moments when she'd been abducted. If she'd known some self-defense, would it have helped? Would Brent and Melody have had a chance?

"Okay, I'll take some lessons."

"We can start tomorrow."

"Actually, I'm not tired. Can we start now?"

He eyed her, then nodded. "Get changed. Kaira showed me a well-equipped gym near the living quarters."

They walked to the suite they were sharing. It had two bedrooms off a small living area. The furniture was utilitarian and a boring beige, but the space had some interesting pictures on the walls. They were photographs of military aircraft, and close-ups of the landscape around Woomera. A lizard on a rock, a tree growing sideways out of a bolder, a flat, desolate salt plain.

Finley didn't own much in the way of activewear, but she had some leggings, T-shirts, and a pair of running shoes. She did like to walk when she got the chance, to clear her head when she'd been working too hard.

Sabin was still in his black, sleeveless uniform. He led her to the gym just down the hall. Lights clicked on, illuminating lots of torturous looking equipment, and a large area covered with mats and bounded by a mirrored wall.

She gave a mental snort. Who wanted to look at themselves while they were hot, sweaty and red in the face?

Sabin stopped in the center of the mat.

Why did the man have to look so damn good? She held her arms out. "So? Where do we start?"

"You need to know where to attack a Kantos." He

circled her. "They're not human. They have different weak points."

"Okay."

"Most Kantos are covered in a hard carapace. Don't bother with a hit to the back—" his hand touched her back "—or chest." He circled around, his fingers brushing her sternum.

Finley gasped, sensation flowing through her.

"Kantos' weak points are their soft spots. Underbelly, joints, eyes."

She nodded.

"If you kick, don't bother with precision. Just try to kick and connect with your shin. It's larger. Hit hard, hit fast. And aim for those weaker spots."

"Shin, hard and fast, weak spots. Got it."

He waved a hand. "Kick me."

"What? I can't."

A smile curled his lips. "You can't hurt me."

Challenge fired in Finley's blood. She rushed forward and kicked, but he blocked her foot with his hand, his reflexes lightning fast.

His hands stroked her calf, setting off small explosions in her belly before he let her go.

"Try again. Harder this time."

She kicked again and he blocked again, swatting her away.

"Harder."

She growled. She swung her leg back and kicked hard. This time she struck his thigh.

"Better," he said.

Except the blow vibrated almost painfully up her body. The man was made of rock.

Suddenly, he moved fast, his big arms wrapping around her from behind. He pulled her back against his hard body.

"Now what are you going to do?" he said in her ear.

She wriggled, and struggled, but she couldn't budge him.

"Remember those soft spots."

With a hard jerk, she got one hand free. She reached up, trying to hit his eyes.

"Good. You'll always be weaker. You need to use your best weapon, your brain."

Hmm. She half spun, and pressed her face to his shoulder. His purple-black gaze met hers. Finley bit her lip and his gaze dropped to her mouth, the purple strands in his eyes glowing.

"Finley." His voice was husky.

Using the moment of distraction, she elbowed him in his gut. It wasn't exactly a soft spot. Still, he grunted, and his hold loosened a little. She kicked his shin and he cursed.

She broke free and grinned. "I did it!"

He came at her in a rush. She gasped and took several steps backward. Then she tripped and fell on her back. A second later, his big body was on hers, caging her to the floor.

Heat washed over Finley.

"Now what?" he murmured.

"Now you kiss me," she said.

He made a tortured sound. "Finley—"

"You're driving me crazy." She cupped his rugged face with her hands. "Don't pull away, Sabin. Please."

"I can't do this. Shouldn't risk losing my control like this."

She closed her eyes. "Of course. I'm sorry—"

His hand closed around the base of her throat and she gasped. The purple filaments in his eyes glowed brightly. "I can't seem to say no to you. Or stay away."

His mouth covered hers.

Oh, God. *Oh, God.* His tongue delved into her mouth, and she wrapped her legs around him. She undulated against him and kissed him back.

Sabin growled and kissed her deeper. Then he broke the kiss, lifting his head. He pressed his forehead to hers.

"You have no idea how much I want you," he said.

His words cut through her belly. No one had ever wanted her like this alien warrior. Then in a lithe move, he rose.

"Come on. It's time for bed." He pulled her up. "Alone. We both need some sleep."

"You're afraid of me. Of this."

He touched her jaw. "No, I'm afraid of myself."

CHAPTER EIGHT

S abin strode down the red, dusty track. The Australian sun was hot on his skin. It was more intense than it had been at Space Corps Headquarters. A small lizard darted across his path—it was tiny, and covered in lots of bumpy scales.

"See that small, rock outcrop ahead?" Kaira pointed.

He eyed the outcrop. "I see it." The petite security commander was keeping pace beside him.

"That's one of the auto turret placements. We have several of them dotted across the complex. They automatically open when there's an attack."

Good. They'd been here for three days, and he'd been busy assessing the Woomera security, and working with Kaira's security team. She'd briefed him on all the security procedures of the large complex, and taken all his upgrades on board.

So far, there'd been no sign of any Kantos assassins.

But it left Sabin twitchy. He'd prefer to face them head-on.

Finley had been locked in her lab most of that time. She was working harder than ever, and only ate and slept when he bullied her into it.

Yesterday, he'd found her asleep on her keyboard. She was pushing herself too hard. He frowned. He didn't like it.

"I almost want the Kantos to try and attack." Kaira's smile was sharp. "I'd like to take a few down."

Sabin detected something in the woman's voice. "You've faced them before?"

She sucked in a breath. "No. My father is...was a Space Corps engineer. He was aboard a ship that the Kantos destroyed."

So much death. "I'm sorry."

She lifted her chin. "Thanks. It was almost a year ago."

Her eyes glimmered, but she shed no tears. Suddenly, her dark eyes widened.

Then she rushed at him, arm raised. Sabin tensed. *What the cren?*

He was readying to defend himself when she swatted his shoulder.

"Got it," she growled.

"Kaira?"

"Sorry." She pulled her hand back.

He saw the squashed bug on her glove. It looked like it had been a spider.

"I saw it heading for your neck. Australia has some of Earth's most poisonous insects. And snakes."

He frowned at the spider's remains. "It's definitely a native species?"

Kaira stilled. "You think it might be Kantos?" She stared at the spider. "It looks normal."

Maybe Sabin was just seeing Kantos everywhere. He pulled out his communicator and thumbed the screen. A security feed to Finley's lab filled the screen. He saw her at her desk, tapping madly at her computer, and it made his chest loosen a little.

He'd upgraded the cameras over the last day and supervised the building of the small safe room in Finley's lab. He'd drilled her on using it—which she hadn't been thrilled about. Being locked in a small space was difficult for her. And anything that took her away from her work left her a little testy.

He smiled. Although, his little *garva* could be testy most of the time. Well, the StarStorm was important, but he'd make sure she didn't overwork herself. She was pushing hard so they could do the test.

"I'd like to schedule some training sessions with your security team," he said.

"Consider it done," Kaira replied.

He liked Kaira Chand. She was very competent, with no grandstanding.

"I think you would make an excellent Eon warrior, Kaira."

She smiled. "I think I'm a bit short."

He returned her smile. "Perhaps slightly. How do you monitor the perimeter?" The Woomera Range Complex covered a huge area.

"It's a large area, with rough, desolate terrain. It's impossible to cover it all by ground. Like I mentioned before, we have sensors in place. We also have a fleet of surveillance drones."

Sabin nodded.

"I won't lie. If a stealthy, alien assassin wanted to sneak in, it would have plenty of opportunity. There's a lot of native fauna out there and they regularly set off the sensors."

He frowned. "Generally, being stealthy isn't in the Kantos playbook. They prefer overwhelming, direct contact. But these assassins are bred for stealth. We have to be ready."

On his communicator, he saw Finley stand. She looked excited, and was talking quickly to the scientists who were assisting her.

Something was going on.

A second later, his communicator pinged.

Finley's face appeared. "Hi."

"Hello," he replied.

"We did it! The targeting system looks good in the simulations." She grinned. "We're ready for a ground test."

"That's great news." He glanced at Kaira. "Finley's ready for a ground test."

The security commander nodded. "I'll coordinate with Dr. Gregson. We should be able to get it set up for today."

When Sabin returned to the lab, Finley was bouncing.

"I feel so good about this," she said.

He touched her jaw and she stilled. Her gaze dropped to his lips and he drew in her scent. He wanted to gorge himself on her.

Thane's words came back to him. Denying himself was as bad as overindulging.

Could he really risk touching her? Risk his control?

"Sabin?"

He blinked. *Later.* Right now, they had a test to carry out.

"Kaira said for you to come to the main observation room."

Finley nodded.

"I am *so* excited," Dr. Gemma Neely said, beaming. The young woman had her blonde hair in two tails that made her look even younger. Ian stood behind the woman, eyeing her with a besotted expression.

Their group headed through a tunnel, and up to the observation room. It was made of solid walls and had a narrow pane of thick glass that gave them a perfect view of the sparse terrain of the test area.

"The lasers have all been set up," Dr. Gregson informed them.

The older woman was standing behind a bank of several computer screens. Some were showing controls for the weapons systems. Others were video feeds of the ground below. Sabin spotted some of the security team out in rugged vehicles near the laser installations.

"Clear the area and prepare for the test," Dr. Gregson said into a small microphone.

Finley was tapping a foot on the floor. Sabin took her hand and she squeezed his fingers.

"Take a breath," he said.

She did. "It's just that this is so important. I want to get to orbital testing."

"Prepare for StarStorm ground test," Dr. Gregson announced.

A timer flashed on the screen. *Ten. Nine. Eight...*

"There are several laser installations. We get this right, they should form a laser net over the test area." Finley smiled. "Then I just need to do it for the entire planet."

...three. Two. One. Initialize.

A flash of bright light. Several of the lasers fired and two met. Then three. A dome-shaped net flowed upward.

"It's working," Finley breathed.

Sabin watched the other lasers fire. The net flowed like water through the air.

Then the next laser misfired.

The beam shot wide and cut into a tree, then a boulder. Rock exploded into the sky.

"Security Team Two, evacuate." Kaira's tense voice on the radio.

"*No,*" Finley whispered. Her fingers clenched on Sabin's.

The lasers all started going wild. On another screen, he saw a security team vehicle racing down a track, a cloud of dust behind it.

Sabin stiffened. They were too close to the lasers.

Finley gasped.

A laser hit the back of the vehicle, cutting through the metal. It skidded to a stop and the doors of the vehicle flew open. Two security officers dove out and ran.

Finley's face went white and she pressed a fist to her chest.

"Roberts?" Kaira barked. "Pascal?"

"We're okay, Commander," one replied.

Finley slumped. Sabin wrapped an arm around her.

The rest of the laser net dissolved, as Dr. Gregson shut down the system.

"Test failure," the computer intoned.

Finley closed her eyes and Sabin felt the tension in her body.

"It's okay, Finley. This is why we test. Failure helps us get it right."

She opened her eyes, and the deep brown looked so empty.

"We don't have time for failure." She pulled away and strode out.

FINLEY STORMED INTO HER LAB.

The test had failed. She'd almost killed those poor security officers.

God.

She smacked the bench with her fist, ignoring the pain that shot up her arm. A tool skittered off and hit the floor.

The door opened, and Gemma and Ian came in. What if they got hurt, too? Around her, everyone got hurt.

"Get out," she said.

They froze.

"Now!"

Both of them spun and the door slammed behind them.

Great, now she was freaking out innocent lab assistants. Devil Delgado was in the building.

Well, she needed to get the problem fixed before the Kantos attacked again. She didn't have time to be nice.

She dropped into the chair in front of her computer. She brought up the systems screen. There was a bug somewhere, or she'd missed something.

The door opened again, and she didn't even bother to look. "I said, get out."

"I'm not as easily cowed as your young assistants."

She looked back at Sabin.

He arched a brow. "I don't think you can force me out, either." A faint smile. "I'm bigger than you are."

"Sabin, I don't have time for chitchat. I have to find the problem—"

He strode toward her, his long legs eating up the space. She tensed.

"You don't have to do it alone," he said.

"My project, my responsibility."

"It's our project now. We'll find the problem together, solve it, and re-test." He rested his hands on her shoulders.

The warmth of his touch felt so good. "What if it fails again?"

"Then we keep working until we get it right."

She looked up. "And if the Kantos attack again? If more people die?"

Sabin pulled her out of her chair and tugged her into his body.

"It isn't on you. You're working yourself ragged. If the Kantos attack again, the Kantos are to blame."

She looked at his chest. It was easy to say, harder to do.

"This isn't just about the Kantos," he said quietly.

A lump formed in her throat.

"It's about your abduction."

"I don't want to talk about it." She could already feel that hot, horrible sensation carving out her insides. She touched her elastic band, fighting the need to use it.

"Okay, but I just want to say, it wasn't your fault your colleagues died. That's on your abductors."

"Do you know how it feels to be the lone survivor? To wonder why you lived, and they didn't?"

He pulled her close, pressing her face to his chest. He smelled good, felt good. She twisted her hands in his shirt.

Would it hurt to lean? Just for a minute?

"You didn't die, Finley, and you aren't to blame for your friends' deaths. The people who took you are." He paused. "You aren't alone."

She made herself pull back. It would be all-too-easy to get used to leaning on Sabin Solann-Ath. But one day, he'd be gone.

"Now, I'm going to let your slightly terrified assistants back in," he said.

She gave him a dry look.

Finley went back to her computer. Gemma and Ian returned, casting wary looks her way. Soon they relaxed and got back to work. Finley lost herself in her work. She pored over the data, picked at the readings from the failed test.

"There's still something off with the targeting," she said.

"Here." Sabin reached over and tapped the screen. "It's in this part of the code. Somewhere."

"You're right." She stared at the screen, but was so aware of him. The scent of him. His face and neck were so close to her.

She turned her head, and her lips brushed his neck.

He stilled, then turned his head. Their mouths were an inch apart.

"Finley, you're driving me crazy," he murmured.

She licked her lips and he groaned.

"I kind of like that," she murmured back.

"Behave," he warned.

She glanced over at where Gemma and Ian were chatting and working.

With great difficulty, she refocused. She pulled her notepad and pen over. Sometimes she needed to write things down the old-fashioned way, and stop staring at the screen. Finley scribbled wildly—every little thing she could think to try.

"Enough."

Sabin's voice made her blink, and she looked up. There was no sign of Gemma or Ian.

Sabin set the tray down beside her. "Eat."

"What time is it?"

"Late. You missed lunch and dinner. I let Gemma and Ian go to bed."

"Right." She rubbed her eyes. Then she grabbed a bread roll and bit into it.

Sabin smiled at her.

She swallowed. "What?"

"You just rubbed ink on your face."

She looked at her hands. Her fingers were covered in black ink. "Oh well, I wasn't planning on entering any beauty contests."

"You'd still win."

Her heart did a little jig, and she made herself take another bite of bread. She didn't taste it.

"You should get some sleep," he said.

"Not yet. I'm close to solving this." She grabbed his forearm. "Please, Sabin. I'm on the right track, I can feel it."

He frowned at her. "Okay. One more hour."

"Thank you, Commander Bossy."

He ignored the jibe. She ate some fruit off the tray and they kept working. This was it. She was sure the tweaks would work.

She pulled her stash of marshmallows out of the drawer. She needed some extra fuel.

"What are those?" Sabin eyed the sweet treats dubiously.

"Marshmallows. The greatest food ever invented." She stuffed a pink puff of gooey sweetness in her mouth, then tipped the bag toward him.

He took one gingerly and squeezed it. Then he put it in his mouth. His face twisted.

"So good," she said.

He grimaced. "So sweet."

"I know." She gobbled another one.

Sabin just shook his head.

With a grin, she licked her fingers and got back to work.

The next thing she knew, Sabin was lifting her into his arms.

"What?" She blinked, her mind foggy.

"You fell asleep on your computer again," he growled. "Bedtime."

Him carrying her was so nice. She snuggled into him. "Okay."

"I like you like this," he said.

"Sleepy?"

"Sweet and agreeable. Of course, I like you prickly and abrasive too."

Her belly did a warm swirl. No one, apart from her family, had ever really liked her just as she was.

"I think I fixed the targeting issue," she said.

"Enough work for tonight."

"We can test again tomorrow."

He opened the door to their quarters. "Okay, Finley, but shut it down for tonight. You *will* rest, and tomorrow, we'll worry about your test."

"Okay, Sabin." Just this once, just for a moment, she'd lean on him.

CHAPTER NINE

"What's taking so long?" Finley tried not to fidget or storm outside to get the laser test ready herself.

She'd barely slept—excited, worried, running everything through her head. The test *had* to work this time. It had to.

"They're repairing the damaged laser," Sabin said. "It shouldn't take too much longer."

It was already past lunch time. She glanced at the clock, then looked back out the narrow window of the test room. The hot, Australian sun was high in the sky. She paced across the test room, glancing at the screens.

Sabin grabbed her arm. "Relax."

"I can't."

He pulled her closer and her heart did a funny jerk in her chest.

"Sabin—" She glanced at the door. They were currently alone, but anyone could walk in at any moment.

His strong hand slid along her jaw. "I'll have to help you relax."

She made a sound. Instantly, all she could think about was him.

His mouth lowered, hovering over hers. "I hate seeing you worried and stressed."

"I'm often worried and stressed."

"Not if I can help it." His mouth took hers.

Oh boy. Her knees felt like they'd melted. He took his time, kissing her thoroughly, like he couldn't get enough of the taste of her.

She slid her hands into his hair and moaned into his mouth.

Finally, he lifted his head, leaving her feeling bereft.

"I can hear Gemma and Ian coming," he said.

Crap. Finley stepped back and ran a hand over her hair. All she wanted to do was jump him.

"You look less anxious." He smiled.

The door opened, and her assistants tumbled in, talking a hundred words a minute. Somehow, Gemma was oblivious to Ian's obvious adoration.

Finley turned to the window, sure the fact that Sabin had kissed her senseless was written all over her face.

"S-Man," Ian said to Sabin. "I'm sure we've got it this time. You and Dr. Delgado are unstoppable."

She and Sabin shared a look.

"I'm feeling confident too, Ian," Sabin said.

Dr. Gregson bustled in. "We're ready." The scientist headed for the control panel.

Finley clasped her hands and tried not to fidget.

It was going to be fine this time.

Sabin stepped up beside her. His hand brushed her lower back. "Breathe."

She sucked in a shaky breath.

"Initializing the test," Dr. Gregson said.

The familiar countdown flashed on the screen. *Ten. Nine. Eight...*

Finley took a deep breath.

...seven. Six. Five. Four...

Another breath. *Please work.*

...three. Two. One. Initialize.

The lasers fired.

She grabbed Sabin's hand and held on tight.

Come on. Come on.

More lasers fired, and the net formed. She held her breath.

"Laser net formation complete," the computer intoned.

She stared at the net, glowing bright under the sunlight. *It worked.* Elation filled her.

Cheers erupted in the room, and Sabin spun her around and hugged her.

The others rushed her, and she found herself engulfed in more hugs.

"It worked," she said.

"It did." Sabin touched her hair. "Congratulations, Dr. Delgado."

"Thank you, Security Commander Solann-Ath. For your help, your belief, and for looking out for me."

Something moved through his eyes. "My pleasure, Finley."

God, feelings were alive inside her. She wanted this strong, fascinating alien warrior.

She cleared her throat. Dr. Gregson came over, grinning from ear to ear. "Congratulations."

Finley nodded. "Thanks for your help with the test. Now, when can we arrange for the orbital tests?"

The scientist's face turned serious as she considered. "It'll take a few days. We need a team in orbit to assist, and not all the satellites are operational yet."

Frustration ate at Finley.

"We need that time to prep down here anyway," Sabin said.

She nodded, fighting the need to move faster.

"I'll keep you informed," Dr. Gregson said.

"I know what we need," Gemma exclaimed. "A party!"

Finley frowned. *A party?*

Ian whooped. "Yes, in the dining room. I'll ask the cooks to make something special, and we'll unlock the bar." He wiggled his eyebrows and flexed his hands. "I am the cocktail king."

"It's an excellent idea," Dr. Gregson said. "We deserve to celebrate the test's success."

Finley frowned. "I'm not sure—"

"Everyone's been working hard."

Sabin raised a brow. "You Terrans don't need much excuse for a celebratory get-together."

"Tell me about it," Finley grumbled.

"And everyone needs to dress up," Gemma added. "Ladies should be in little dresses."

Finley frowned. "I didn't bring a dress." She'd come here to work, not party.

And not lust after a certain alien warrior. That wasn't going according to plan, either.

Gemma stepped in front of Finley, the young woman eyeing her with a critical look. "Laura from the missile guidance lab is almost as tall as you. She'll have something you can borrow."

Sabin looked like he was fighting a smile. "I need to contact my ship and update my war commander. I'll see you at the party."

The traitor abandoned her.

"Come on." Gemma dragged Finley out.

An hour later, Finley stepped into the dining room, having been primped within an inch of her life. Everyone was drinking and eating. Some were dressed up; others were still in lab coats and wrinkled jeans.

Finley wished for her lab coat. She was wearing a borrowed, blue dress that was an inch shorter than she'd like. It wrapped across her body and had a deep V-neck, and left her legs bare. She'd brought some cute sandals with her, so at least she was wearing her own shoes. Gemma had done her makeup, but Finley had balked at letting the woman do her hair. She'd just brushed it out and left it loose. The blonde color looked nice with the blue.

"Dr. Delgado, the woman of the hour." Ian, wearing a horrid, red bow tie, pressed a huge, ball-shaped glass into her hand. "I made this just for you."

It was a clear liquid with pineapple and a sprig of green on the side. "What is it?"

"A gin cocktail. I called it the StarStorm in your honor. Drink up."

Gingerly, she took a sip. Mmm, it was tasty.

She scanned the room. There was no sign of Sabin.

She took another sip.

What the hell, she may as well relax a little. Right now, there was no more work she could do. And no sign of the Kantos. So, she was going to enjoy herself.

SABIN HEARD the happy noise of the party as he walked down the hall. He'd touched base with Malax, and his gut was still hard.

They'd had news of the Kantos. The aliens had invaded a planet in a system not too far from Earth.

Reports said that entire cities and villages had been decimated. The planet, C'addon, had been peaceful. The C'addonites spent most of their days building temples and worshiping their goddesses.

Now they'd been wiped out and consumed by the Kantos.

The insectoids wanted to do the same to Earth.

He wasn't going to let that happen.

Trying to shake off the bad news, he entered the dining room. He looked around, searching for Finley.

He passed over a tall blonde, then his gaze zeroed back. His chest locked.

By Eschar's embrace. She wore a form-fitting dress the color of a jewel. The flirty skirt left too much of her long, silky legs bare. He hadn't known her legs were that long. The neckline gave him a very nice view of the swells of her breasts.

His body responded. His helian pulsed.

He struggled for some control. A deep inner urge wanted to grab her, take her away, and spend hours exploring every inch of her.

He'd come here for the mission, but inside, he knew Finley was his, too—at least for now. At least until he could get her out of his system.

She turned her head and smiled. He strode through the party, ignoring Dr. Gregson as the woman tried to talk to him.

Finley turned. "Parties are supposed to be fun, Sabin. You're scowling like you saw a Kantos."

"What are you wearing?"

"A dress." She touched the hem. "What's wrong with it?"

He leaned close and lowered his voice. "You look too good in it. I don't want any man looking at you except me."

Pink tinged her cheeks. "They aren't looking."

"I can assure you they are. At your long legs, your elegant shoulders, the swell of your beautiful—"

"Sabin." She lifted her chin, pressing one hand to his chest. "What's gotten into you?"

He breathed in her scent and it enflamed him. "You."

Her chest rose. "They can look, but they can't touch."

"Can I touch?" he whispered.

She licked her lips. "I want you to."

Cren. Desire was like a hot blade to his gut. He couldn't let it take him over.

"Dr. Delgado." Gemma appeared. "We need you to solve an argument about inertial confinement fusion." The woman glanced at Sabin. "I'll bring her back."

Sabin dragged in a breath. As the woman towed Finley away, she glanced back over her shoulder, her brown eyes heated.

"Here, have a beer." Kaira appeared and shoved a drink into his hand. She was wearing wide-legged, black pants, and a fitted, white shirt that looked good with her brown skin. "You'd better stop looking at the doc like you want to throw her over your shoulder and drag her off to a dark corner." The commander grinned and sipped her beer. "Or a big bed."

Feeling a little desperate, Sabin took a gulp of his drink. It was bitter, but had an interesting flavor. "I...have been fighting the attraction."

"Why?"

"I'm here for the mission. To get the StarStorm operational."

"Sabin, I'm guessing you won't let anything stop your mission. And your feelings for Finley motivate you even more to keep her safe, and complete the StarStorm."

"Eon warriors don't usually mix missions with pleasure." He couldn't afford the risk.

Kaira snorted. "How many humans are now mated to Eon warriors? All while battling the threat of the Kantos?"

He tipped the drink toward her. "A valid point."

"If you're attracted to her, and have feelings for her, that's special. Honor it. Enjoy it for as long as you have it.

You never know when it might get yanked away." She looked away. "Gone forever."

He cocked his head. "Kaira?"

She released a breath. "I lost my husband two years ago."

She'd lost two important men in her life so close together. How devastating. "I'm sorry."

"He was in the Air Force as well. He died in a training accident." Grief crossed her face. "I was lucky to have Ryan as long as I did. We were married for two wonderful years. He was a good man."

"I hope, in time, you meet another," Sabin said.

Kaira shook her head. "We have a saying on Earth that lightning never strikes twice." She straightened. "Anyway, this is a party. We should be having a good time." She touched his hand. "Don't waste the time you have with her."

Kaira's words, the echo of her grief, rattled through his head. Could he live without ever knowing Finley's touch? Was she worth the risk to his control?

He turned and watched Finley smile at something Gemma said.

The Kantos were coming. She was their target.

Don't waste the time you have with her.

Driven by the need inside him, he said goodbye to Kaira and moved toward Finley. He grabbed her drink and set it on a nearby table.

Her brows creased. "Sabin—?"

"Come with me."

She followed without a word. Already so much trust between them.

He led her through the corridors, and up some stairs. He opened the door that led to the roof.

"Oh," she breathed.

Stars filled the sky overhead. He led her over to a spot where someone had left some chairs and a blanket laid out. Clearly, some of the scientists came up here when they needed fresh air. He'd found the spot when he'd assessed the building security.

"Look at the stars, Sabin." She arched her head. "I can't believe you travel through them."

He'd become so focused on his work, he often forgot how beautiful space could be.

"I have seen some amazing things." His gaze was on her as she smiled at the sky.

He reached for her and pulled her down on the blanket. They both lay back and she rested her head on his arm.

"Look." She pointed. "A shooting star."

"It's not really a star," he said.

"I know that, but we have an old tradition of calling them that and making a wish." She closed her eyes.

Right then, Sabin wished for so many things, all centered around this woman.

He rose up on one elbow and leaned over her. Gently, he pushed the strap of her dress down and kissed her shoulder.

She shivered. Her beautiful, intoxicating scent filled him. He dragged his lips over her skin, pulling in all the sensations.

Her hand slid into his hair. "Sabin."

Need filled him—hot and vicious. He pushed the top of her dress down.

She wore another froth of delicate lace on her full breasts. He lowered his head and sucked nipple and lace into his mouth.

She moaned and arched into him. He took his time, savoring, then moved to the other breast. She was a temptation he couldn't keep away from.

"So pretty, Finley. And sexy."

"Really?" She was breathing fast.

"Yes." He shifted, his hard cock pressing against her hip.

Her lips parted, hungry need in her eyes.

"Where do you want me to touch you?" he asked.

"I—"

"No." He pressed a finger to her mouth, shaped her lips. "Show me."

She was frozen for a second, then her gaze roamed his face. Her hand moved, sliding down her body. Over the silky fabric of her dress.

He growled and his cock pulsed.

She grabbed handfuls of the skirt of her dress, bunched it up, baring more thigh.

Cren. He felt wild. A male predator sensing a female.

Finley's hand slid between her legs. She made a husky sound.

"There?" he asked.

"Yes. I feel empty, hot. Sabin—"

He moved his hand to join hers.

He found matching lace panties. "These are in the way."

"I can—"

With one hand, he gripped the lace and yanked it off. They tore easily.

"*Oh.*" She jerked.

Then he twined his fingers with hers, and together they stroked the sleek, soft folds between her legs. She moaned, and he bit back a curse.

So soft and wet. The scent of her arousal was driving him wild.

She writhed. He explored her, stroked. He slid her finger and his inside her tight warmth.

"Sabin. *Please.*"

He bit back a growl. He lifted his hand and licked, the taste of her exploding in his mouth. *More.* He needed more.

He pushed her hand away, feeling like a wild beast. He shoved her legs wider apart.

Then his mouth was on her.

Finley's cry pierced the night. He licked, sucked, and lapped at her. Her legs locked around his head. The feel, the scent, the warmth of her swamped his senses.

"Oh, God, yes. Sabin, *please.*"

He found the small nub with his tongue and she went wild. He sucked and she broke apart. Her body shook and she cried out his name.

Sabin had never felt need like this. He wanted her so badly his hands were shaking. His senses were spinning out of control.

She fell back on the blanket, panting. Her gaze locked on his face. "Sabin?"

His body shook as he fought for control. Fought not to pin her down and take everything he wanted.

"Sabin." Her hand cupped his cheek.

"Don't touch me. My control...isn't good right now."

She sat up and cupped his other cheek. "It's not supposed to be. Together, like this, I don't want your control."

"I don't want to hurt you. I don't want...to lose myself."

"You won't." Her voice was firm, certain. "I trust you, Sabin. You're one of the steadiest, strongest people I've ever met." Her lips touched his.

The kiss was slow, deep. The desire twisted hard inside him, but it was tempered by his need to pleasure her, to keep her safe.

He pressed his face to her neck, heard the fast beat of her heart and his own. "Finley—"

Then his communicator chimed.

Sabin cursed the interruption. He didn't want to let her go, didn't want to lose this moment. He took a second to touch her face, and flipped her dress down. He yanked out the communicator and Kaira's face filled the screen. She looked grim.

"Sabin, perimeter sensors in the north went off. The drones spotted something, but it's blending into the shadows. It doesn't look native, but it's hard to tell."

For a second, Sabin fought to think through his desire.

"I'm on my way." He ended the call and pulled Finley up.

"I need to—"

"Go. I know. Go."

He cupped her face. "We have unfinished business."

She smiled. "I'm feeling great."

"And I'm hungry for more." He kissed her. "Now, get inside. I want you safe."

CHAPTER TEN

The rugged vehicle bumped along the rough track.

The darkness was thick, and even with his helian-enhanced vision, it was hard to see much. The lights of the vehicle speared ahead, highlighting the rocky ground.

"We're getting close." Kaira was in the driver's seat, driving expertly, her hands clamped on the wheel. Two of the security team sat in the back, one manning the large gun mounted on the back of the vehicle. "Turning headlights off."

They plunged into utter darkness. Kaira pulled on night vision goggles, and Sabin did the same.

"Anything?" Finley's voice came from his communicator.

He glanced at the screen. She looked worried. There was no sign of the sweet passion she'd showed him on the rooftop.

"Not yet," he replied.

The vehicle was electric and made no sound, other

than the crunch of the tires on rock. Finally, Kaira pulled them to a stop.

"We'll go in on foot from here." She touched her ear. "Pascal, anything on the drone feed?"

"Nothing, Commander."

"I need to turn the communicator off now," Sabin told Finley. "I'll leave audio on."

Finley nodded. "Be careful."

Sabin climbed out of the vehicle and formed a blaster with his helian. He followed Kaira and her security officer, Roberts. The final man, Blackwell, stayed back with the vehicle.

They were alert to any sounds or signs of movement.

"I'm detecting several tiny life signs," Sabin said.

"A lot of the native wildlife is nocturnal. Sensors have been going off a lot in this area."

They kept moving.

Suddenly, something dropped out of the sky.

Sabin tensed.

"Watch out," Kaira bit out.

A small animal fell and hit the dirt. It lay there, unmoving.

Kaira crouched and flashed a small light. It was a bird. Sabin saw white feathers and a splash of bright yellow.

"Native bird. Cockatoo. It's dead." With the tip of her gloved finger, she tipped the bird over, then sucked in a sharp breath.

Its eyes were hollowed out, and thick, sticky mucus covered its face. It oozed from the dead bird's mouth.

Roberts made a gagging sound.

"Something's definitely wrong with it." Kaira stood. "Kantos?"

"Maybe," Sabin replied.

With an unhappy look, Kaira jerked her head and they kept moving.

Soon, she glanced at the rugged watch on her wrist and then stopped. "We're at the location."

The three of them fanned out. There was no movement. Sabin didn't detect anything.

He turned in a slow circle, and then felt a faint ping on his senses. His helian flared.

"East," he murmured. "I'm detecting a larger lifesign."

"Form up," Kaira murmured.

The three of them moved together, staying close. Sabin heard a skitter of rocks and shadows moved.

They all whipped their weapons up.

"I can't see a thing." Kaira crept forward. "You?"

"No."

There was a burst of movement in the shadows.

"Left!" Sabin yelled.

Something large darted away.

Cren. Was it an assassin? He couldn't tell.

He leaped over the rocks and skirted a tree. Kaira's officer tripped and cursed.

Sabin slowed to a walk. There was no movement, but something was watching them. He felt it.

Suddenly, a creature burst out from some rocks, bounding across the ground.

Kaira let out a low laugh.

"What the *cren* is that?" Sabin asked.

"A wallaby. A native animal." The creature bounded on its strange legs and disappeared into the darkness.

"What the fuck?" Kaira muttered.

Sabin swiveled. She was looking into a shallow gully. The younger officer caught up with them. The young man was panting.

Sabin followed Kaira's gaze. He saw more dead cockatoos first. They littered the ground.

Then he stiffened.

The bottom of the gully was filled with...eggs.

They were large—twice the size of his head. They sat upright, and looked to be a dark brown, but it was hard to tell in the darkness.

"Jeez, it's like a sci-fi horror movie," Roberts whispered.

"How the hell did they get here?" Kaira said. "We should have seen them."

Sabin glanced at the birds. "They used the birds, somehow. Your sensors detected the birds, but that didn't raise any red flags. The eggs probably haven't been here long."

"Recommendations?" Kaira asked.

Sabin ground his teeth together. "They need to be destroyed." This meant the Kantos were here, somewhere. *Cren.* "I suggest fire."

Kara nodded. "We'll get the flamethrowers out of the truck—"

Before they could move, one egg slowly opened with a faint cracking sound. The top unfurled, and a spindly leg climbed out. Then another.

A small Kantos spider, about the size of Sabin's palm, perched on top of the egg.

"Oh, shit." There was fear in the officer's voice.

Another spider climbed out of the same egg.

More eggs started opening.

The first spider leaped into the air and Sabin fired on it. It exploded.

A second one leaped, and Kaira shot it with her blaster.

All around them, more spiders climbed out. Too many.

As a group, the Kantos bugs moved, skittering forward across the ground.

Sabin, Kaira, and the officer all started firing. A spider leaped at Roberts and clamped onto the man's face. He screamed.

On his other arm, Sabin formed a knife. He kept firing his blaster, and reached out and sliced the Kantos off the man. The creature shriveled and hit the rocks.

The young man stumbled back, panting.

"Keep it together," Sabin barked. And fired again. "Kaira, cover me."

The woman nodded, still firing and not taking her eyes off the spiders.

They were heaving along the ground, moving like a living blanket. Sabin ran up a small rocky outcrop. He morphed his blaster into one that cast fire.

A spider leaped at him and he caught it, and crunched it between his fingers. He kicked another.

Then he aimed his newly formed flamethrower into the gully. He shoved the night vision goggles off his face.

"Kaira, you and Roberts stay back. Night vision goggles off."

Flames spewed, lighting up the night.

The spiders screeched in an eerie howl. Fire poured over the spiders and the eggs. Several of the aliens tried to leap out of the way.

Kaira took them down with precision shots.

Soon, the stench of burning flesh filled the night air. Before long, the egg patch was a smoking ruin.

Sabin leaped down off the rocks.

And in the darkness, he saw them.

Three—no, four—Kantos assassins.

He froze, and saw the stalker bugs restlessly sitting by them. With the flap of wings, the assassins took to the night sky. One remaining assassin from the first team, and a second team.

Their hunting bugs leaped away into the darkness.

They were heading toward the base.

Finley.

"Kaira!" Sabin turned and started sprinting. "Four assassins and their stalker bugs are headed toward the base."

"Fuck," the security commander muttered.

"Vehicle! *Now.*"

The three of them sprinted back toward the vehicle that Kaira called an SUV. They leaped in and she started the engine, yanking on the wheel. Rocks flew from under the tires as they pulled in a tight turn.

"What's happening?" the officer on the turret called out.

"Kantos assassins," Kaira yelled back.

They sped down the track, the vehicle bumping along. Sabin almost hit his head on the roof.

Kaira yanked sharply and they came out onto a wider track. She picked up speed.

Sabin grabbed his communicator. "Finley!"

"Sabin?" Her frantic face appeared on screen. "Are you okay?"

"We're fine. We found the Kantos. Finley, you need to lock down the base. Tell Kaira's team to lock down."

"What?"

"Tell them to follow lockdown procedures." That meant they would get the scientists into the secure underground labs. No one would be able to get in or out. He took a deep breath, just as they hit a huge bump.

Behind him, the turret fired.

"There are four Kantos assassins heading your way," Sabin said.

Finley went pale. "If we lock down, you won't be able to get in."

"We can take care of ourselves. I want you safe. You're the target."

"Enemy spotted," the officer on the back of the SUV yelled. The turret gun fired again.

Sabin looked out the window and spotted the flap of wings in the sky.

Suddenly, the gunfire cut off, and the officer on the turret screamed.

"Blackwell's gone!" Roberts yelled.

Cren. "I have to go, Finley," Sabin said. "Lock down and stay safe."

She pressed a finger to the screen. "You, too."

FINLEY CHEWED ON HER NAIL, listening to the gunfire over the communicator.

"We need to get down to the underground labs." Dr. Gregson was tense. "Once we initiate lockdown procedures, reinforced doors will close. No one can get in or out."

"But Sabin, Kaira, and the others won't be able to get in, then?" Finley's gut churned. "We can't leave them."

"They're well-trained, Finley. The security commander wants you safe."

Reluctantly, Finley nodded. With one of Kaira's security officers and the other scientists, they started trudging down towards the labs. Her fingers tightened on her tablet, listening to the fighting.

Please be all right, Sabin.

They walked quickly down the corridor. One more level, and they'd be inside the safe zone.

She looked out the window. All she saw was darkness, but she knew out there, somewhere, a fight was raging.

Then she saw movement and froze. "Something's right outside."

Everyone stilled, fear on their faces. Gemma was as pale as a sheet. Finley stepped closer to the window, and saw a stalker bug step into the glow cast by a security light. She sucked in a breath.

"A Kantos hunting bug," she said. "If it's close, so is its assassin."

"Hurry," the security officer urged.

They picked up the pace, Finley's sandals clicking on the tile floor.

Suddenly, a large form crashed through the window.

Gemma screamed and glass sprayed everywhere like deadly rain.

The assassin landed in a crouch in front of them, its wings flapped open.

Gemma screamed again.

"Get back," Finley yelled.

Ian grabbed Gemma. Her group started walking backward.

The assassin lifted its head. Its many eyes seemed to look right at Finley.

"Run!" she screamed.

She spun and ran. She sprinted down the hall, the others stumbling along. The security officer aimed behind them and fired.

Together, they turned a corner.

The assassin's wild screech echoed off the walls.

Finley glanced back. The alien turned the corner, moving fast.

Dammit.

She looked around. A plant in a large, ceramic pot sat against the wall. Its leaves were brown and crispy, so she guessed no one had been looking after it.

She snatched it up. As the Kantos rushed at her, she tossed the plant.

The pot hit the assassin in the head, and the creature staggered. The security officer fired on it again.

Finley tried the nearest door. Locked.

Come on, give us a break.

She tried the next one, and it opened.

"In here!" It was a lab. There were several experiments lined up on the benches.

Her group hurried in and she slammed the door shut. "Quick, help me move this."

She gripped a cabinet that was shoved against the wall, and Ian and the security officer moved up beside her. Together, they all pushed. They shoved it in front of the door.

Suddenly, the door shuddered under the weight of the impact of something massively heavy.

"Oh, God." Gemma sagged against a bench. "It'll slaughter us all."

"Gemma, there will be no slaughtering." Finley swallowed. The pounding on the door increased. It wouldn't hold up much longer. "It's after me. All of you, lock yourselves in the office." She pointed to an open door on the other side of the room, through which they could see the corner of a desk covered in papers.

"No," Ian said. "We aren't leaving you to be bait."

"There's no need for all of us to die."

"Fuck that," Dr. Gregson bit out. "We need some weapons."

"I'm out of ammunition," the security officer said.

The door burst open, the cabinet crashing to the floor.

The assassin stalked in, wings snapping open.

Gemma whimpered.

Finley backed up, her hand running over the bench, searching for anything that she could use as a weapon.

There were beakers, test tubes, a chunky machine for testing that was far too large to lift, a Bunsen burner.

Shit. The assassin leaped, its wings flapping.

Finley ducked and scrambled under the bench.

She leaped up on the other side, and spotted several scalpels and some other tools resting on the bench. She snatched them up and threw them at the Kantos assassin.

One scalpel pierced the creature's wing, and it jerked.

"Hey, asshole." Ian leaped up on top of a bench, clutching a bottle in his hand. He tossed it at the creature.

The glass smashed, and some sort of liquid chemical sprayed the alien.

The assassin screeched. The liquid was eating into the alien's wings.

"Ian, more." Finley grabbed all the vials she could. She pelted them at the assassin. The rest of the group started grabbing bottles and beakers, and throwing them at the alien.

"We're probably going to kill ourselves," Dr. Gregson yelled.

"Better to explode than death by *that* thing," Ian answered.

The Kantos screeched again and slipped, crashing to the floor.

Gemma grunted. "Help me."

Finley saw the younger woman pushing against the large testing machine. Finley raced to help her. If they tipped it off the bench, it would land directly on the assassin. The others rushed over to help. Together they all shoved hard, and the machine inched toward the edge of the bench.

"More," Gemma urged between gritted teeth.

Finley strained.

The machine reached the edge of the workbench, and then gravity took over. The heavy machine dropped off the edge, right onto the assassin's torso.

The creature went silent, its legs twitching, then it stilled.

Finley pressed her hands to her thighs, sucking in air.

"We did it," Gemma said, incredulously.

Ian laughed. "Oh, my God."

"We did it," Dr. Gregson cried.

They all started laughing and hugging each other. Finley slapped Gemma on the back. Then she heard the sounds of screams and gunfire. *Sabin.* She yanked out her tablet.

"It's right above us," Kaira yelled.

"Kaira, look out!" Sabin shouted.

Finley's heart leaped. Then she heard the crunch of glass and metal, and a man's scream.

"Sabin? Sabin?" There was no answer. "Where are they?"

Dr. Gregson blinked. "I don't know—"

"You have drones. We need the footage. *Now.*"

"Hang on." The woman raced to the nearest computer, tapping some keys to wake the screen. She started clicking away. "Got it!"

The screen filled with aerial footage, tinged green by the night-vision setting. Finley's pulse pounded madly.

The footage zoomed in, and she spotted the overturned SUV. It was on its roof.

"*No.*" It felt like the floor beneath her caved in.

She couldn't see any sign of Sabin, or the others. Something flew between the drone and the SUV. An assassin.

"They're five hundred meters away from the main building," Dr. Gregson said.

Finley pressed a hand to her head, trying to think. Then she saw something move out of the darkness.

One of the stalkers. Then another. And another. They advanced on the wrecked SUV.

"We have to help them," Finley said.

"Finley, it's too dangerous," Gemma said.

"Sabin wanted the base locked down," Dr. Gregson added.

"Then you guys lock down. I'm going to help them." Fear was alive in her belly, but she wouldn't abandon Sabin, or the others.

"I'll come with you," Kaira's security officer said.

"Me too." Ian stepped forward, chin lifted.

Finley nodded. "Let's move."

CHAPTER ELEVEN

Pain rocketed through Sabin. He groaned.

He felt the wet slide of blood down his side. He was hanging upside-down in the vehicle, and the windshield was shattered. He turned his head and saw Kaira beside him, caught up in her own belt. She wasn't moving. But when he strained, he heard the beat of her heart.

"Roberts?"

There was no answer from the back.

Then Sabin heard a low screech outside.

Cren.

He formed a knife on his arm but his helian was sluggish, too focused on healing his injuries. He clumsily slashed and cut the belt, and his body dropped. He shoved against the mangled door and managed to climb out.

He glanced down and saw metal sticking out of his skin. *Cren.* He was bleeding badly. He was about to pull the piece of debris out of his side when he detected movement.

Not far away, three stalkers eyed him, slinking closer, their antennae quivering.

Cren. He let the knife morph into a sword. He had to protect Kaira and Roberts.

The first bug leaped.

Sabin lunged and slashed with his sword across the Kantos. It hit the dirt with a spray of green blood.

The others shifted uneasily.

Where were the assassins? He couldn't risk checking the sky, because as soon as he took his gaze off the bugs they'd attack. He hoped Finley was locked down and safe.

A second bug darted forward. He swung his sword and dodged. Its mandible snapped together.

Sabin shifted again, and pain roared through his injured side.

A stalker charged.

Sabin sidestepped, and brought his sword down.

The bug screeched and raced away. He'd hurt it, but it wasn't a life-threatening wound. The others had disappeared into the darkness.

Wincing, he gripped the metal chunk in his side and yanked it out. He groaned, fighting to stay conscious.

The injured bug eyed him, clearly sensing his weakness. Then, he heard a noise behind him.

He glanced around and saw a third bug circling around, heading toward the vehicle. Coming after Kaira and Roberts.

"Get away!" Sabin leaped over the tangled ruin of the

vehicle and slammed his sword down. He skewered the bug and it wriggled on the blade.

He reached over and wrenched the door off the side of the SUV, then stopped to fight off a wave of dizziness.

He reached in and cut Kaira free.

Gripping her arms, he pulled her out, ignoring his pain. He lifted her, gritting his teeth, and set her on top of the overturned vehicle. Next, he reached farther in and pulled an unconscious Roberts out of the back.

He glanced over and saw that the injured bug was watching, waiting for something. Probably the assassins.

Then he heard a noise in the darkness. A skittering sound.

He hefted Roberts beside Kaira.

Sabin saw the first spider. Then another. Then another. He raised his sword and gritted his teeth.

A wave of spiders marched out of the darkness.

To borrow an Earth word, fuck. He leaped up onto the vehicle.

There wasn't enough strength in his helian right now for him to form any flames. The spiders surrounded the overturned vehicle. Sabin closed his eyes for a second, and Finley's face filled his head. Her smile, brown eyes, the furrow in her brow when she concentrated.

Pain throbbed, and he ground his teeth together.

A spider flew at him and he sliced it with his sword.

More flew up and his sword became a blur as he fought them off. The endless wave of them kept attacking. And more rushed out of the darkness.

He couldn't stop all of them before they'd overwhelm him.

Or before he lost too much blood.

One spider landed on his shoulder and bit.

Sabin roared at the sensation, fire burning his skin.

He slapped it away, and then sliced several more.

Suddenly, he heard the roar of an engine. He glanced over and saw light spearing through the darkness.

The vehicle sped into view, then skidded to a stop.

He saw Finley behind the wheel.

No.

He'd wanted her safe.

The doors of the vehicle opened and he watched Ian and another security officer get out. They were holding bulky weapons.

Finley climbed out, then clambered onto the hood of the vehicle. She also had one of the bulky weapons in her arms.

"Fire!" she yelled.

Flames spewed from the weapons. The mass of spiders quivered and tried to escape. Finley and the others waved the flamethrowers around, fire lighting up the night.

Earsplitting screeches filled the air. The Kantos spiders writhed and shriveled into small husks.

Finley jumped off her vehicle. Sabin saw movement behind her.

A stalker.

"Finley!"

Sabin leaped into the air. He sailed over Finley and landed, pain flaring in his chest.

The hunting bug leaped.

He swung his sword, but missed. His reflexes were slow.

The bug slammed into his chest and they hit the dirt. The bug attacked, tearing and scratching at his chest.

"Sabin, no!"

All he felt was pain. Then Finley was there, hitting the bug with a stream of fire.

It fell off Sabin, curling up into a charred crisp.

"Oh, God. Oh, God." She dropped down beside him, gently touching his wounds.

"Fin-ley."

"Shh. Let me help you." She turned to the others. "Are the Kantos gone?"

"I think so," Ian replied shakily.

"Sabin's hurt. We need to get him back to base."

"A-assassins," he managed to get out.

She glanced up. "We killed one earlier."

"More."

She bit her lip, determination filling her face. "Guys, we need to move, there might be more assassins. Get Kaira and her officer into the vehicle."

The men nodded and disappeared from view.

"Finley—" Sabin groaned.

"Quiet." Her hands stroked his hair. He saw fear in her eyes as her gaze skated over his wounds. "Stay still and quiet."

She lowered her head and pressed her lips to his. "This time, I'll save you."

The spider poison was burning in his veins. His helian was doing what it could, but the pain was driving him closer to unconsciousness. He groaned.

"Help me shift him," Finley said.

He must have passed out as they moved him. He came to in the vehicle with his head resting on Finley's lap.

"Get us back as fast as you can," Finley called out. "Sabin said there are other assassins still out there."

Sabin tried to move but his body wouldn't obey.

"Stay still." She stroked his cheek. "You're going to be okay. I promise."

FINLEY'S HEART was in her throat as the security team carried the stretcher with Sabin on it into their quarters.

They lifted him onto his bed. He'd lost consciousness on the drive back.

Her stomach felt like a hard ball. He'd be okay. He had to be.

For a second, she had flashbacks to her captivity. Brent had been beaten to the point of death. He'd been so hurt and in so much pain.

She squeezed her eyes closed and took some deep breaths. She couldn't lose it.

"I can send the medic," a security officer said.

"No, they're busy with Kaira and Roberts. I can take care of Sabin."

The man gave her a quick nod. "Don't worry, Commander Chand is as tough as steel. We've locked down the base, so we're safe for now."

Finley swallowed. "Any sign of the other assassins?"

"There's been nothing on the security feed."

"Thank you."

After they left, she hurried into the adjoining bathroom, and grabbed a bowl and a cloth. She filled the basin with steaming water, and carried it back to the bedside table.

Sabin had a jagged wound on his side, and slashes from the hunting bug on his chest. There were holes all through his scale amor, and skin showed through.

She swallowed the lump in her throat. She needed to get the armor off him so she could treat his wounds. She touched it. The scales were tough, but flexible under her fingers.

She felt the warmth of him.

He was alive. That was all that mattered.

She slid her hand along his arm. "Sabin, I need you to retract your armor."

There was no response.

She touched the thick band that housed his helian. It pulsed and she stroked it. "I need his armor off so I can help him. We can help him together."

She felt another pulse, then the black scales started to flow off his skin, retracting back into the band.

Her heart did an extra thump. Then she saw the full extent of his injuries and nausea rose in her throat.

Swallowing back the ugly taste in her mouth, she reached for him. "Sabin." He must be in agony.

Finley got to work cleaning the blood off him. The horrible bite on his shoulder was turning black at the edges. As she washed it, he stirred.

"Shh." She pressed a kiss to his forehead.

She went over to his large, black bag and rummaged

around in it. She found a small container and pulled out a vial of *havv*.

She hugged the vial to her chest. "Thank God."

She sat on the bed. She tipped *havv* onto the wound on his side, then the scratches, and then the bite. She smoothed the red fluid across his skin.

He stirred, his muscles tensing. She stroked the hair off his forehead. Then she rinsed out the cloth and wiped down his face.

"I'm here. I'm not leaving you."

He was still restless. She kicked off her shoes. She was still wearing her borrowed dress—although it was looking a little worse for wear—but she didn't want to leave him to change. She found a black shirt in his bag— made of silky Eon fabric. She quickly slipped off her dress and bra, and pulled the shirt on.

Tiredness and worry pulled at her. She ran a shaky hand across her face. She checked his wounds again and thought they maybe looked less inflamed, but they were a long way from healed.

He thrashed a little on the bed.

"It's all right, Sabin."

At the sound of her voice, he settled, his face turning her way.

She stroked his jaw and then climbed onto the bed beside him. She moved to his uninjured side and lay down next to him.

Warmth pumped off him. She pressed a hand to his flat abs.

"I don't like seeing you hurt, warrior. Seeing that SUV crashed and overturned..." Her throat tightened.

"Heal now." She snuggled into his side. She wasn't sure who needed the comfort more, him or her.

She set her watch alarm to ring in two hours, so she could check on him. Then sleep dragged her under.

It felt like seconds later when her alarm beeped, and she fought off sleep. She sat up and checked his wounds in the low light of the lamp she'd left on.

His scratches were healing well. She blew out a breath, relief a wild rush inside her. The bite mark was almost gone. The wound on his side was deeper; it looked better, but it still wasn't healed.

She brushed her fingers over his cheek and he turned his face into her palm. With her other hand, she touched the helian band.

"Rest, Sabin."

Finley fell asleep again, pressed against him. When she next checked him, she could barely pry her eyelids open. She was exhausted.

But the scratches on his chest were just pink marks. The Eon *havv* was amazing stuff.

She fell asleep once more, cocooned by his warmth.

When she woke next, it was because something was tickling her cheek. She made an annoyed noise and turned into the pillow.

But her pillow was warm, firm, and hard.

She opened her eyes.

Sabin was up on one elbow, leaning over her.

"Are you okay?" She moved to sit up, but he pushed her back down.

His face was unreadable. She scanned his chest.

And only saw pristine, bronze skin.

The air shuddered out of her.

His hands circled her throat, his thumb on her pulse point. Her pulse jumped at his caress.

"I recall telling you to get to safety, and to lock down the base," he said, in a low voice.

He was angry with her? "I saved your life, and you're angry?"

He leaned down closer. "Because it's your life that matters. You raced into danger, and the Kantos could've killed you!"

His voice turned to a yell.

Finley's anger ignited. "Well, your life matters to me!"

He stilled. The purple in his eyes glowed. "It's my duty to protect you."

"Well, I'm protecting you right back, Sabin." She shook her head. "I couldn't let you die."

He growled. "Finley."

"Be mad, but I don't regret it. Seeing you healed and whole—" she met his gaze "—was worth every risk."

He stilled. "You undo me." His voice was deep, husky.

"Sabin—" Heat flooded her belly.

He lowered his head, his mouth on hers. Then she wrapped her arms around him and kissed him back.

CHAPTER TWELVE

S abin drew in the taste of Finley.

By the warriors, he wanted to drown in her, imprint himself on her.

He made himself lift his head. "I need to shower." His wounds were clean, but he still felt the gore and dirt of the fight.

Her lips curved. "I'll join you."

His cock throbbed. *Cren.*

She rose. She was wearing his shirt, her long legs bare. His hands flexed. He wanted to tear the fabric off her and put his mouth and hands on her.

With a smile, she turned and walked into the bathroom. He heard the shower turn on and he followed, his heart drumming in his chest.

In the bathroom, she pulled the shirt off. She glanced at him and lifted her chin. Almost defiant.

He remembered what she'd said, that she was too tall and too large to be beautiful here.

"You are gorgeous." He let his gaze drift over her. "Magnificent."

Her teeth sank into her lip. "You make me feel like that." She stepped into the shower, her gaze on him.

He took his own clothes off until he was naked, cock hard and rising. He needed her and he could no longer fight it.

He stepped into the shower stall, and she watched him, hunger in her eyes.

They moved under the water together. Her hair was a slick fall down her back, shades darker than it was when it was dry. She reached out and squirted some soap on her hands, then rubbed it against his chest. As she touched him, he realized she was checking his now-healed wounds.

"I'm fine." He still needed to eat, his energy was low, but his wounds were fully healed.

She pressed a kiss to his chest.

He'd never wanted or needed someone like this before. Never had someone cared for him as she did.

Her soapy hand slicked over his body. He gripped her waist, one hand shaping her curvy buttocks. Her hands circled his cock and he groaned.

She stroked him, touched him until Sabin couldn't think past the beat of desire. He circled his arms around her and lifted her. She gasped.

"I love your strength," she murmured. "I know you'd never hurt me."

Her trust in him made him believe it. He pinned her to the tiles and kissed her. Then moved his mouth down her neck as she wound her long legs around his hips.

He found one breast and sucked the nipple into his mouth.

She moaned—a sweet sound. Sabin took his time as the water cascaded over them, locking them in their own little world.

He moved to her other breast. By the stars, she was so beautiful.

"Sabin." Her voice was needy, her hands digging into his shoulders.

He turned off the water and carried her out. He sat on the bed, with her straddling him.

"We're wet," she said.

"I don't care." He leaned forward and licked the water off her skin.

"Oh, that feels good," she moaned.

"I want to make it feel even better. Will you let me love you, Finley?"

Her chest hitched. "Yes."

She reached between them and found his cock. He groaned.

"You're so big." She stroked him. "I'm not very experienced or good at sex."

"This requires two people, Finley. You can't be bad at it alone."

He took her mouth again and their tongues tangled. He stroked a hand down her body, over her belly and into the curls at the juncture of her thighs. He stroked.

"*Oh.*" Her hips shimmied

"I need to check to see if you're ready." He wouldn't hurt her.

"I'm ready any time I look at you."

He felt intense satisfaction at her words. She was wet, and moved on his hand. He thumbed the small nub of her sex. "Like that?"

"Yes." Her voice was breathless.

"Do you want my cock inside you, Finley?"

"Yes."

"I'll give you anything you want." He wrapped his hand around hers on his cock. "Come here."

His voice was a growl. She rested her hand on his shoulder, and together, they held his cock as she positioned herself over him.

She pressed down.

As the swollen head of his cock lodged inside her, they both groaned.

"Sabin—"

Cren. "Go slow. You're tight."

"It's been a while." She bore down, her teeth biting into her lip. "And you aren't small."

Slowly, her body opened and took him. Sabin was shaking, fighting the need to plunge into her.

Finley made a sound, and in one swift move, she sank down, taking the rest of his cock.

"*Finley,*" he growled, his hands digging into her hips.

She threw her head back.

He leaned forward and raked his teeth down her neck. "Are you all right?"

"Oh, yes."

Her gaze met his. Her hips lifted, then sank down.

Raw desire was like fire inside him. She was like a fist clamping around his cock.

"I feel like I've wanted you forever." His fingers clenched on her curves. "Move, my *garva*."

He buried a hand in her wet hair, and set his teeth on her neck again.

She moaned, her hips moving faster as she rode him.

He heard her harsh intakes of air, the scent of her arousal. They rocked together and Sabin thrust up, wanting nothing between them. He wanted to be as deep as possible inside her.

"Sabin, *Sabin*."

Her inner muscles rippled on his cock. Her nails scored his back.

"Right here, Finley. I'm ready to watch you come." His finger found her clit. "Feel how hard I am for you."

"Just for me?"

"Yes, now come." He pinched her clit and thrust up, his cock deep.

With a scream, she came. Her movements turned jerky and she rocked down on him.

With a roar, Sabin rose and turned. He slammed her onto the bed and thrust hard inside her.

His release hit him like a blinding white light. His body shuddered hard and he growled her name.

He poured himself inside her and she wrapped herself around him—arms, legs, her inner muscles.

Sabin buried his face in her hair and felt at home. His port in the darkness. His harbor from the storm.

FINLEY WOKE facedown on the bed, feeling good.

So good.

Lips pressed to her spine, traveling down her body. Her belly clenched.

"What time is it?" She couldn't get used to being underground with no windows.

His teeth scraped her spine and she bit her lip. Sensation rocketed in every part of her body.

"Early," he responded.

He sank his teeth into her bottom and she shuddered. A pulse beat between her legs. She was a little sore, but she wanted him again.

She turned on the bed and pressed a kiss to his chest. Sabin smiled at her and then his mouth met hers. He cupped her cheeks, and kissed her like she mattered.

Careful, Finley. She pulled back. His eyes were warm, but his face was drawn.

She cupped his cheek, feeling the rough stubble under her fingers. "Are you okay?"

"I just need some sustenance. My helian expended a lot of energy healing me."

"Oh!" She pushed away. "I'll get you something to eat."

"No." He pulled her back down on the bed. "Stay here. Naked. I'll get it."

Finley lay back and watched him leave the bed. God, the man was delectable. There was no sign that he was self-conscious being naked. Why should he be? As he walked across the room, she drank him in. He was all solid muscle, strong thighs, and a gorgeous ass. She shivered. As he walked out the bedroom door, she had the perfect line of sight as he raided the fridge. She watched him eat quickly and efficiently. He brought them both back a protein drink.

She took hers and moved to cover herself with the sheet.

"No." He stopped her. "I like looking at you."

She fought a blush. "I've never eaten naked with anyone." She cocked her head. "I've never eaten naked at all."

As she drank, he cupped her breast. He played with her nipple until it was a hard point.

"Sabin."

He finished his drink in one last gulp and set the glass down. He took hers, and set the glass beside his, then he kissed her.

She moaned against his lips. She nudged him back and then remembered his horrible injuries. "Let me check your wounds."

"You know I'm fully healed."

"I'd like to see for myself."

As he lay there, she ran her hand over his shoulder. There was no sign of the bite mark. She kissed the smooth skin. Next, she moved to where he'd been scratched. She peppered kisses across his pecs.

"Finley—" His hands snaked into her hair.

She found his flat nipple and licked, before she nipped it with her teeth.

He groaned.

She felt a sense of power to affect a man like Sabin in this way. A strong, disciplined alien warrior. She moved lower and pushed him back. She found his healed side, the skin perfect. She raked it gently with her teeth and then went lower.

"I wasn't injured there," he said.

She smiled against his hipbone and cupped his cock. *Oh, boy.* She licked the head of it.

He jerked and whispered her name.

Finley licked again, then sucked his hard cock into her mouth. It pulsed against her touch and she sucked as much of him as she could. She savored the salty taste of him. She really enjoyed his tense body, every single one of his reactions. She could feel the way he savored every sensation.

"I won't last much longer." He yanked her up his body.

"I don't mind."

"I'm not coming down your pretty throat, Finley. I want to be deep inside you."

Her belly spasmed. "Sabin—"

He pushed her onto her back. He kissed her knee, her thigh, her belly. His tongue dipped into her belly button. She arched up, then his big body was over hers.

Oh, he was gorgeous. She'd never get tired of looking at him.

"Everything about you feeds my senses, Finley. Your scent, the sound of your voice, the feel of your skin."

She quivered. No one had liked any of those things about her before.

"How your body takes me inside you." He sat up, his big hands circled his cock and pumped.

Oh. God. Liquid heat washed through her. Watching him touch himself was so hot.

"Sabin, *please.*"

"You need me?"

"Yes, please make the ache better."

He leaned over her, and rubbed the head of his cock against her folds. She cried out.

"There." He covered her, then with a single thrust drove inside her.

"Sabin!"

"*Finley.*" A deep groan. "I could stay inside you forever."

He pulled her legs tight to his sides. She held on as he thrust inside her. It was hard, deep. He took over every part of her.

As his thrusts got harder, she pressed her mouth to his skin. He filled her up, surrounded her. Right here, right now, she wasn't the sensible, and sometimes lonely, scientist. She was just Finley, a woman who needed this man. This man, who made her feel desired. Protected.

Her body spasmed. She was close. "I want you to come with me, Sabin."

He slowed his thrusts but they were still deep, his gaze locked on hers.

The feel of him was mind-blowing, touching places in her no one had ever touched.

She gripped his big biceps. "Sabin, please. *Together.*"

"We are together, Finley." He changed the angle of his hips. "Just you and me."

Her release built like a wave, rising higher and higher. A searing orgasm rippled through her.

Finley's scream was hoarse. As pleasure swept

through her, she held on tight to this man who made her feel so much.

He moved faster again. *"Finley."* A growl and a prayer.

Then his big body shook as he came inside her. His grunts were the sexiest thing she'd ever heard.

Sabin dropped down beside her, moving them so his cock stayed lodged deep inside her.

"Perfect." He pressed a kiss to her shoulder.

She fought back tears. She'd never been perfect. She'd always been too smart, too big, too tall, too difficult. She swallowed and realized that Sabin meant it. To him, she was.

God, when this alien warrior left her, he'd shatter her heart.

CHAPTER THIRTEEN

Finley finished dressing, and tied her hair up in a ponytail.

She turned to find Sabin right behind her. He was in his usual black uniform. He slid an arm around her, his hand resting on her butt as he pulled her close.

His kiss lit up everything inside her. He'd touched, stroked and kissed every part of her through the night.

As they pulled back, she drew in a breath. "Enough. We need to meet the others."

He stroked her lips with his fingers, then let her go.

Of course, he'd left her blood humming. As they walked down the hall, she was sure anyone looking at her would know exactly what she and Sabin had spent the night doing. She glanced at him. She was so damn grateful that he was all right.

The horror and fear of the night rose like a specter, her throat tightening.

Frowning, Sabin glanced at her. "What's wrong? I can sense your distress?"

"I'm just glad that you're okay."

He slid an arm across her shoulders. "I am, too, but if you put yourself in danger again like that, there will be trouble."

He dropped a kiss to her hair.

They met the others in her lab.

Kaira rushed forward. "You're both okay?" The Air Force commander had a bandage on the side of her head.

"We're all right," Sabin said. "You?" He eyed her bandage.

The woman nodded. "Just scrapes. Roberts and I are fine." Her lips firmed into a flat line. "We recovered Blackwell's body. I've informed his family of his death."

"I'm so sorry, Kaira," Sabin said. "I know that it's not easy to lose a member of your team."

She lifted her chin. "The Kantos will pay."

"Any sign of them?" he asked.

"We have extra drones up in the air, but not a single sighting."

Finley bit her lip. *Where the hell were they?* There were several assassins still out there, somewhere.

Sabin crossed his arms over his chest. "They're out there. We'll find them."

Dr. Gregson nodded. The older woman looked tired. "I sent Admiral Barber an update on the attack last night. She's moved up the orbital testing."

Finley straightened, her pulse jumping. "Really?"

The woman nodded. "They've moved a Space Corps orbital team into position. We'll do the testing today."

Finley gasped. "Today?" She glanced at Ian and

Gemma. "We have so much to do." She looked at Sabin. "We have to get prepped."

"I want to check on base security with Kaira," he said. "I'll meet you back here soon."

Finley nodded. As the others left, she got busy. She needed to get the testing satellites in position. This *had* to work.

She pressed her hands to the workbench. They needed the StarStorm operational. Yesterday.

For a second, she had a flashback to driving out to the crashed SUV, not knowing if Sabin was alive.

Damn, she was falling for him.

So stupid, Finley. Sabin was an alien warrior. An Eon warrior. She knew that he was dedicated to his ship and empire.

And she knew he liked to keep control of his senses. This attraction between them threatened that.

She pressed her fingers to her temple, feeling a headache forming. The fact that he would leave didn't change how she felt. No one had ever made her feel like he did.

She'd enjoy every minute she had with him until he left. She straightened. She'd make every moment count. For however long she had him.

She turned to her computer. "Gemma, check the firing sequence."

"On it, Doc."

This test would be more challenging in orbit. There were so many new variables to account for. As she ran through the testing program, worry chewed at her.

She felt a touch on the back of her neck and blinked. Sabin smiled down at her.

"You need to make more noise when you move," she muttered.

He smiled. "I don't think you would've heard a starship arrive."

"We need this to be ready for the test—"

He squeezed her shoulders. "We'll be ready."

As Sabin moved over to a second computer, she triple checked all her calculations. Sabin started checking the targeting.

Dr. Gregson arrived. "Are we ready?"

Finley blew out a breath. They were as ready as they'd ever be. "We're ready."

"The orbital team is in position," the woman said. "Send them the coordinates, so they can get the satellites in position."

Finley sent the data through. A big screen on the wall flickered to life, and the image displayed the interior of a small Space Corps shuttle, with the orbital team aboard.

Behind them, she saw half a dozen satellites out in space.

"Moving the array into position," came the deep voice of one of the astronauts.

Finley fidgeted. Sabin touched her waist and she grabbed his hand. She didn't care who was watching.

They watched the astronaut leave the ship. He wore a sleek, black-and-white spacesuit with a streamlined helmet. He flew gracefully through space until he reached the first satellite. He opened a panel, adjusting something on the control panel.

"This is Storm Team One. The satellites are in position."

Finley blew out a breath. This was it. She watched the astronaut return to the shuttle.

"Initializing StarStorm orbital test," a female voice said.

Finley's mouth was dry now. The Kantos were coming. They wouldn't stop. They *had* to get the Star-Storm working.

But she couldn't help but feel like she needed more time. That they were rushing things.

The countdown started.

She held on to Sabin's hand.

"Oh my God, my nerves are killing me," Gemma said, from behind Finley.

The first laser fired.

Finley sucked in a sharp breath. It looked so different in space.

More lasers fired, the net forming.

"It's working," Ian said.

Finley's chest expanded. The net was beautiful.

"The final laser is failing to fire," the female voice said. "But the others are successful."

Gemma squealed and hugged Ian. His cheeks went red. Finley turned to Sabin and grinned.

"Just one small glitch, but it worked."

"Congratulations," he said.

Finley squealed and threw her arms around him. He lifted her off her feet, then his mouth was on hers.

She didn't care about the others, she just kissed him back. His tongue stroked hers and he took his time.

When they lifted their heads, Gemma and Ian were grinning at them.

Finley fought a blush, but she didn't care.

For however long she had him, Sabin was hers. She'd cherish every minute.

He set her on her feet.

"The test was a success," Sabin said.

"But one laser failed. We still need to do some fine-tuning."

"Let's get to work."

"*AHH.*"

Sabin lifted his head and watched Finley throw her old-fashioned notebook across the lab. It hit the wall, then smacked to the floor. She slumped in her chair.

"Finley?" It was just the two of them. Gemma and Ian had worked with them all day, but left for the evening an hour before.

"This was supposed to be an easy fix," Finley said. "But I can't do it all from down here." She blew out a breath.

Her jaw was tight and her shoulders stiff. He walked to her, and massaged her shoulders. "You have a team to help. You don't have to do every little thing yourself."

She grunted. "I need the orbital team to manually adjust some of the weapons systems."

"So send them the instructions."

"This isn't their specialty, and the StarStorm is completely new. What if they get it wrong? What if—?"

"They get it right." Sabin crouched in front of her. "I know this is your project. I know you feel a great sense of responsibility." He rested his hands on her thighs. "You are not alone."

"I know."

"Send the instructions."

"Now?"

"Yes. So you don't stress and stew on it."

She huffed out a breath, then tapped on her computer. Finally, she hit send.

"There. Detailed instructions sent to the orbital team." Her computer chimed and she leaned forward to read the message. Her lips quirked. "They're going to start work right away."

"See?" Sabin stroked her thigh.

Her gaze dropped to his hand and lingered.

"You can relax now," he said.

"Hardly. I'll still worry about it. And if the damn Kantos assassins attack again..."

Sabin had seen the mess of the fight with the assassin in the other lab. His gut clenched. She could so easily have been killed. Ian had detailed the fight for him and how courageous she'd been.

His. Sabin's helian pulsed. She was his to care for. To protect.

He stroked his hand higher and she stilled. He flicked open the button of her sensible pants.

"Sabin." Her voice was half shocked, half aroused.

"I want you to relax."

"Anyone could come in—"

"Everyone is gone for the night. They were

exhausted trying to keep up with you." He stroked his fingers along the seam of her pants and she gasped. "Do you like that, Finley?"

"I like any time you touch me."

He gripped the sides of her pants and tugged. She clutched the arms of her chair and lifted her hips. "Sabin, if someone does walk in—"

"I locked the door when Gemma and Ian left."

She licked her lips. He knelt in front of her and slid his hand up her bare legs.

"Touch yourself," he said.

Her cheeks turned pink, but she slid her hand down her body. She had a sensual streak she kept hidden.

His blood pulsed, his cock surged. "I love looking at you."

She touched herself and moaned softly.

Desire roared higher. Sabin pushed her hand away, then leaned down and put his mouth on her.

"*Sabin.*"

He licked and sucked, watching her writhe under his touch. He loved pleasuring her.

She panted, whispering his name. A hand slid into his hair, holding him to her.

"Oh, *yes.*" Her body shook as she came.

Sabin slowed his kisses. He pressed a kiss to her inner thigh and she shivered.

Then he pulled her out of the chair, lifting her into his arms, making sure her lab coat covered her lower body.

"Sabin, my trousers—"

"I've got them." He carried her out of the lab. "Now I'm taking you to bed."

She slid her arm across his shoulders. "To sleep?"

He grinned. "Eventually."

In their quarters, he took his time stripping her. He wanted to savor, not to rush. They'd done fast, now was the time to indulge. To touch, taste, and stroke every part of her. When they were tangled on the bed, he moved inside her—slow and deep—their gazes locked together.

They came together, her crying out his name as he groaned out hers.

They fell asleep, naked, and wrapped in each other.

It felt like only minutes later that his communicator chimed.

Sitting up, Sabin turned on the bedside lamp. He saw that they'd been asleep for several hours. He grabbed his communicator. It was a call from Malax.

"Sorry to wake you, Sabin," his war commander said.

Finley sat up just out of view, and pushed her hair out of her face. She stayed quiet.

"It's fine, Malax."

"You're all healed?"

"Yes. And there's been no sign of the Kantos."

"I wish I could say the same." Malax's face was set. "What's the status of the StarStorm?"

"We're close. The orbital testing went well. The Space Corps astronauts are making some adjustments."

"We're out of time," Malax said.

Finley stifled a gasp.

"What's happened?" Sabin demanded.

"The Kantos fleet is headed for Earth."

Sabin bit back a curse. "How long do we have?

"I'm en route with the *Rengard*. The other closest Eon warship to Earth is the *Valantis* and they are coming, too. We won't beat the Kantos. You have twenty-four Earth hours before they arrive."

Now Sabin cursed. Finley bit her lip.

"One Kantos battlecruiser has gone missing," Malax added. "We don't know where it is."

The news just got worse and worse.

"We'll do what we can to prepare," Sabin said.

"Get the StarStorm ready, Sabin, or Terrans will die."

The screen went blank and Sabin tossed the device onto the bedside table.

Finley crawled across the bed, and wrapped her arms around him. He held her tight.

Their time had run out.

CHAPTER FOURTEEN

The next morning, Finley paced the lab, waiting for the astronauts to call in.

"What's taking so long?" she snapped.

Everyone was packed into her lab and ignored her. They were all tense.

"Woomera Complex, this is Storm Team One."

Finally.

Dr. Gregson touched the screen. "We're here, Team One. This is Dr. Amelia Gregson."

"Sorry for the delay." The man sighed. "My team worked all night, but they were unable to complete all the required work."

"What?" Finley stepped forward.

Sabin wrapped an arm around her and held her in place.

"We just don't have the technical expertise. This project is new tech that we aren't trained on. I'm sorry."

"We've received news that the Kantos are on their way," Sabin said.

"We know." The astronaut's tone was grim. "We need your weapons scientist up here."

Finley sucked in a breath. "Me? In *space*?"

Sabin frowned. "You're certain Dr. Delgado is required?"

"I'm afraid so. My team did the best they could. We all know this project was fast tracked, for good reason, but that leaves Dr. Delgado as the sole expert. We can't complete the final piece of work alone. We need her."

"I've never been to space. I have no training." Panic was a slick, hot slide in her veins.

Sabin gripped her arm. "I'll be with you. Every step of the way."

Dr. Gregson frowned. "Finley, we're out of time and options."

"God." She set her shoulders back. "All right."

She saw a flare of pride in Sabin's eyes.

"We'll send a shuttle to collect you," the astronaut said.

The call ended.

"Well, I guess I'm heading into space." Her stomach did a jittery turn.

Sabin cupped her face. "I'll be with you. Every second."

Before Finley knew it, a Space Corps shuttle touched down on the landing pad in front of the main Woomera building. Her hair was braided, and she carried a small, soft tool kit in her hand, that contained all her gear.

"Good luck." Gemma hugged her. "You've got this."

Ian saluted.

The side of the shuttle opened and a man appeared,

clad in a Space Corps uniform. "Dr. Delgado, Security Commander Solann-Ath. I'm Sub-Captain Malicki." He waved them aboard. "Dr. Delgado, we have a spacesuit for you." He took her toolkit.

Inside, the first thing she saw in the tight space of the shuttle was a black-and-white spacesuit hanging from a hook.

"Lieutenant Watts is our pilot today," the sub-captain said.

A woman waved back at them from the cockpit, sitting in front of a huge panel of controls.

"Get changed," Sabin said.

Finley moved to the most private area at the back of the shuttle. She took off her clothes, then pulled and heaved to get the formfitting suit on. Her curves were *not* designed for space.

The suit zipped up to her neck and felt like a second skin. She ran her hands down her body a little self-consciously. It didn't leave much to the imagination.

When she moved back to the main part of the shuttle, Sabin's gaze lit up. He took her in and smiled.

She touched her side. "It's tight."

"You look great." He leaned in close and nipped her ear. To the pair in the cockpit, it would look like he was just murmuring to her.

She shivered.

"Take your seats," the sub-captain called back. "We're ready for takeoff."

She and Sabin sat, and clipped their harnesses on.

She could do this. The fate of the world was resting on her shoulders. Sabin reached out and took her hands.

He had his scale armor on now. She glanced down. His hand was so much bigger than hers.

"It's going to be fine," he said.

She nodded. She wasn't alone. She knew Sabin would keep her safe, and help her.

The shuttle lifted off. Out the side window, she saw orange dirt and a glimpse of the Woomera buildings, then they speared into the blue sky.

The shuttle sped up and she was pushed back into her seat. She tried to stay calm. Sabin was relaxed. He'd probably done this a thousand times before.

Before she knew it, the blackness of space appeared through the cockpit windshield.

"Oh wow." The shuttle moved into orbit. She looked back down at the Earth. It looked exactly like every photo she'd ever seen, but it was even more incredible.

"We're heading straight for the satellite array," Sub-Captain Malicki called back. "After you've completed your work, we'll rendezvous with the Hurst Space Station."

As she looked out the window, a huge, orbiting station came into view.

"Is that the Hurst?" she asked.

"Ah, no. That's the Citadel low-orbit prison."

That was where Eve Traynor had been wrongfully imprisoned, before this entire situation with the Kantos had exploded. Space Corps had come up with a crazy plan to get the Eon involved, and had forced Eve to abduct an Eon war commander.

Of course, she was now mated to that war commander, and expecting the first Eon-Terran baby. So, Finley guessed it had all worked out.

She glanced at Sabin. She wondered what the mating process was like.

"Approaching satellite six," the pilot said.

Finley leaned forward. She saw the laser satellite ahead. It had a stocky, cylindrical body, with solar panels swinging out on the sides.

"We'll come up alongside, then you'll need to use the air lock to travel across to the satellite and its control panels," Malicki told them.

Finley's eyes widened. "*Wait*. I have to go outside?"

"It's only a few meters," the sub-captain said.

"I've never spacewalked." Her breathing sped up. "This is my first time in space!"

Sabin squeezed her hand. "Look at me."

She met his purple-black eyes. They were so steady and calm.

"You can do this," he said. "You're brave, smart. I've seen you fight Kantos assassins, work until you fall asleep at your desk, solve complex problems. This will be easy."

"And you'll be with me?"

"Right beside you." He leaned closer. "I think you might enjoy it."

She pulled in a shaky breath. "Okay, let's do this."

SABIN LISTENED to the airlock door control cycle and beep. Finley stood beside him and he sensed her nerves. She was tapping one foot against the shuttle's floor.

He held her hand and his gaze dropped. Her space-suit hugged the sweet curves of her ass. He swallowed a groan. He needed all his focus. This was an important mission. That, and keeping Finley feeling safe and relaxed.

He stroked a hand down her back. "Ready?"

"No."

"You'll do fine. Try to enjoy yourself."

She made a strangled sound as the airlock doors opened.

Sabin wrapped an arm around her as they pushed off. They floated out of the shuttle.

"Oh, God. Oh. God." She held on tight.

"Breathe."

"I'm breathing."

He looked at her through her helmet. "Finley, open your eyes." She had them squeezed shut.

She opened them. "Oh."

He maneuvered them in the direction of the satellite. "Look at the planet you're protecting."

She looked down at the blue orb of Earth. Sabin had to admit that was a hell of a view. The planet was beautiful.

"Wow." Her fingers clenched on his.

He pulled her, using his helian to help maneuver them. She laughed, delight in the sound.

He let her go and spun onto his back.

She was smiling through her helmet and she reached for him. Their bodies bumped together.

He held her to him. "This gives me ideas. And you in that suit..." He made an appreciative noise.

She smiled. "Stop it."

"Come on." He took her hand again and moved toward the satellite.

They reached the main body of the satellite, their hands pressed to the metal.

"I need to access the main control panel," she said.

They shifted around the main body.

"There," she said.

Sabin pulled open her little pack of tools. They reached the panel, and he used a tool to open the door.

The inside was filled with an array of blinking lights.

Finley pulled out her tablet, which was now resting in a heavy-duty case, and plugged it in. She got to work.

"I need to reprogram the system." And just like that, she lost herself in her work.

Watching her, he smiled. He was pretty certain she'd forgotten he was there, and that they were currently floating in space above her planet.

He loved that about her. The way she threw herself into her work and got absorbed.

She muttered to herself and his chest locked. He was falling hard for this smart, unique Terran.

As she worked, he scanned around. He wondered how his security team on the *Rengard* was doing. He glanced at the solar panels on the satellite, and frowned. They were draped with strange, glimmering strands.

"Almost there." Finley smiled through her helmet, distracting him for a moment.

Sabin glanced back at the solar panels. He moved closer and touched one of the strands with his gloved hand. It stuck to his fingers.

Like a spiderweb.

He felt a skitter of unease.

"*There.*" Finley pulled back with a nod. "Let me just test the laser components."

"Okay." Sabin turned his head, searching for any other signs of the Kantos.

Maybe he was just jumpy. This could be something left over from construction of the satellite. It was highly unlikely the aliens could've been here without the Terrans noticing. Although Terran technology was still far behind Eon technology.

"All right, starting the test...now."

He watched the lights on the panel flicker and dance.

"All readings are within parameters." She touched her tablet screen. "Wait!"

"What's wrong?"

"I've got a high-temperature reading in zone three." She frowned, tapping quickly.

"What does that mean?"

"I'm not sure, but something isn't right." She grabbed her tool. "I need to dig a little deeper." She opened a secondary panel inside the first one. She hummed a little. "Everything looks fine. Let me open a few more internal panels."

Sabin looked at the solar array again and frowned. The back of his neck was prickling and his helian pulsed twice.

Suddenly, Finley gasped.

"What is it?" he asked.

"I'm...not sure."

He moved in close. Behind one of the internal panels, a gelatinous mass oozed out. It was brown in color.

"That's not part of the satellite." It wasn't a question.

"No," she said.

He touched the substance and his helian recoiled. "I think it might be Kantos."

"*No.*" She shook her head. "That's not possible."

"They know about the StarStorm. They targeted you. It's not surprising to think that they might try to sabotage the satellites."

An alarm screamed through their helmets.

"There's a temperature rise in the satellite." She swiped and tapped the screen. "I need to get it under control, or it's going to blow."

"Dr. Delgado! Security Commander." Malicki's urgent voice. "We're detecting a temperature spike."

"We see it," Finley barked.

Sabin watched as the gel inside the satellite started to glow orange.

"Finley, we need to go."

"No. I have to fix this. We can't lose the laser."

The orange goo was now turning red. The alarm screeching in their earpieces increased, as did Malicki's frenzied warnings.

"Finley, we need to go now!"

"Sabin, I—"

The satellite exploded.

He heard Finley scream, but he was thrown back by the force of the blast, tumbling over and over in space. "Finley!"

CHAPTER FIFTEEN

Finley was spinning over and over. She thought she was screaming, but maybe it was just in her head. She was too terrified to make a sound.

She couldn't control her spin. She couldn't stop. Everything was a blur.

She tried to touch the controls on the arm of her suit, but she'd only had a quick lesson and couldn't remember what buttons to press.

All of a sudden, she jerked to a violent halt. She smacked against Sabin's chest.

"Finley, I've got you. Are you okay?"

She was breathing too fast, the sound echoing inside her helmet. "Sabin?"

"You're all right, now." His strong arms closed around her.

As she started to calm down, she spotted the shuttle close by, near the damaged satellite.

"The fucking Kantos," she snapped.

Her fear morphed into anger. They'd destroyed the satellite.

"Your helmet is cracked." Sabin ran a finger down the thin line across the helmet.

It was a hairline crack but her stomach clutched. *"Space will be fun, Finley. You'll enjoy it."*

Despite the circumstances, Sabin flashed her a quick grin. Then he checked her suit controls.

"It's holding. Let's get back to the shuttle."

That sounded like a damn good idea.

He took her arm, and there was a puff of air from his armor. They started toward the shuttle.

Suddenly, there was a blinding flash of light.

Finley bumped into Sabin, and heard him curse. Ahead, a wall of brown filled her vision.

She blinked. *What the hell?*

She took a second to realize it was the hull of a ship. Her pulse spiked.

A giant ship. A long, bulbous body, with several protuberances that looked like legs. The ship was shaped like a bug.

Oh, shit.

The legs on the ship started to glow, and it suddenly fired. The shuttle exploded.

"No!" Malicki and his pilot.

Sabin pulled her close. There was no way for them to get away.

But Sabin tried.

He maneuvered them away from the Kantos ship, using the propulsion his helian generated. They picked up speed, flying into the dark of space.

Finley's heart was beating so hard it hurt. She noticed the crack in her helmet had widened. *Oh, God.* Everything had gone to hell. She didn't tell Sabin, not wanting to distract him.

She glanced back and saw the huge bug-shaped ship bearing down on them.

"What is it?" she asked.

"A Kantos battlecruiser. One had gone missing."

"I guess we found it."

A large hatch on the bottom of the vessel opened. It moved closer, looming over them.

Then it swallowed them.

Finley clung to Sabin, trying to fight back her terror.

The hatch shut, and there was a whoosh of sound. Gravity clicked in, and they dropped to the floor, no longer weightless. She was trying not to hyperventilate.

Sabin helped her up. Wherever they were, it was dark and silent.

"The atmosphere is fine." He helped her take off the damaged helmet. His own retracted.

"Sabin—"

In the darkness, his fingers brushed her cheekbone. "We're together. I'll do whatever I have to do to keep you safe."

Her throat was tight, but she nodded.

Lights clicked on, bright beams, spearing into her eyes.

As she threw up an arm, she heard a chittering noise. She grabbed Sabin's hand.

Several bugs came out of the darkness, and into the circles of light.

Then she saw the Kantos soldier.

It had four long, jointed legs, a strong torso made of a hard, brown shell, and two sharp, blade-like arms held out in front of it. More Kantos soldiers came out of the darkness. Sabin stiffened, and her stomach coiled.

This wasn't good. This was the opposite of good.

One of the soldiers moved forward. It was paler than the others, a little taller.

We want all your information on the Terran weapons system.

The alien was talking in her *head*. She gripped Sabin's fingers harder. It felt like an invasion. This had to be a Kantos elite.

She stared at its four, bright, pinprick eyes. It was looking at her.

Dr. Delgado, you will tell me everything.

"Screw you," she snapped. "I'm not telling you *anything.*" The StarStorm was the only thing between Earth and annihilation.

A Kantos soldier moved forward and raised a sharp arm.

There was a slash of a sword and Sabin moved in front of her. He sliced the Kantos soldier's arm off.

She gasped. Green blood splattered on the floor.

More soldiers raced forward. Sabin fought, taking down another one.

But there were too many. They surrounded him.

The elite moved closer. The next thing she knew, it grabbed her, pressing a sharp arm to her neck. Fear was slick and oily inside her.

Stop.

Sabin saw her and froze. His sword retracted, and the Kantos soldiers hit him again and again. He dropped to the floor.

"No!" she yelled.

They kept hitting him and she heard his pained grunts.

"Stop it!" Finley tried to pull away from her captor.

One of the soldiers slapped something on Sabin's helian band. It was a blob of thick, black gunk.

He lay slumped on the floor, his face swelling from the beating.

Her heart hurt. *Sabin.* Black terror rose inside her. Once again, she was helpless, a captive, watching the enemy hurt someone she cared about.

You will tell me what I want to know.

The Kantos elite swung her around. He pulled her up on her toes.

Or I will torture the Eon warrior until you do.

Her lips trembled and she bit her tongue. She wanted to scream in rage, but she knew it wouldn't help.

I'll give you some time in a cell to decide.

The elite lifted an arm and several soldiers dragged Sabin across the floor.

Another moved forward and shoved her.

How the hell would they get out of this alive?

HE WOKE WITH A GROAN.

Sabin was facedown on the floor, pain throbbing through his body.

There was no sense of healing warmth. He touched his wrist. It was sticky. He couldn't connect with his helian, which left him lightheaded. He tried to sit.

"Take it easy."

Finley.

She was right beside him and helped him sit up. Memories poured in.

They were on a Kantos ship. He shifted and pain throbbed. He groaned. Their cell was small and dank, with sticky lines of something running down the walls.

"You're okay." She pushed his hair back. "I wiped most of the blood off your face." There was worry in her eyes, and she stroked his jaw. "You aren't healing."

"They cut off my connection to my helian."

She stared at the black gunk on his band. "Oh, God."

"Hey, stay calm," he said.

She nodded, but her eyes were wide.

He realized that this had to be her worst nightmare. Held captive, seeing someone hurt.

"They beat you so badly—" Her voice broke.

Sabin hugged her to his chest, uncaring about his aches and pains. He slid a hand into her hair. "I'm tough. My body is stronger than a Terran's."

She nodded against his chest.

"I'm going to get you out of here," he said. "I promise."

"Sabin." She looked up. "They want all the data on the StarStorm."

Cren. "You aren't going to tell them anything."

Her eyes flared. "They threatened to torture you!"

168

He gritted his teeth. "We can't tell them anything. Billions of Terran lives are at stake."

She pressed her hand to her mouth. Then she rose and started pacing. "I can't watch them torture you. I won't."

He pushed to his feet, stifling a moan. He strode to her and yanked her into his arms. "Shh."

"Sabin... I care about you. Please, I can't watch them hurt you."

"Okay, okay." Without his helian, their options were limited. "Then we need to escape."

"Escape?" Her eyebrows rose. "How?"

"When the guards come, we'll take them down. We'll get free, find a ship, and leave."

"Fight them with what?"

"You're smart, Finley. I'm strong, even without access to my helian. We can do this."

He kissed her. Both to calm her, and partly because he needed it.

"Okay," she said against his lips. "We need a plan."

"Let's see what we can figure out."

They made a plan. It wasn't great, but it was the best they could do. Finally, they heard a buzzing in the corridor.

The Kantos were coming.

Sabin prayed to the warriors that there weren't too many of them. "Ready?"

She nodded and dropped to the floor in the center of the cell, sprawled out like she'd collapsed.

Sabin climbed the sticky walls, and held himself

above the cell door. His body ached all over, but he shoved the pain aside.

Finley was the most important thing.

The door opened and a Kantos soldier entered. It paused, looked at Finley, then rushed over to her.

A second soldier stepped inside, and Sabin expanded his natural senses. Even without his helian, he only detected two soldiers.

He dropped. He landed on the soldier and the alien spun.

Sabin gripped its neck and heaved. The soldier spun again and slammed Sabin into the wall.

Cren. Pain exploded through all of him. His vision swam and he fought to stay conscious.

He twisted his hands again and he heard a snap as the soldier's neck broke.

The alien collapsed.

Sabin landed and watched the second soldier turn to face him, its yellow eyes glowing.

Finley leaped onto the alien's back. The soldier turned, trying to reach her.

Sabin knelt and broke off the sharp arm of the dead Kantos. He rose and rushed at the soldier.

"Finley, clear."

She leaped off and hit the floor.

He swung the Kantos arm like a sword. It cracked against the arm of the other soldier. They traded blows, crossing the cell.

Sabin dropped low and whacked at the alien's leg. He aimed for the joints.

With another hard blow, he heard the Kantos soldier's leg crack. The alien tilted.

Sabin went in for the kill.

The Kantos kicked out wildly and hit Sabin's gut. He flew back, winded. His makeshift weapon clattered to the floor.

Cren. He fought back the pain. The soldier straightened, limping forward.

Finley snatched up the arm and held it up. She rushed at the soldier.

She drove it into the alien's eyes.

A buzzing, high-pitched sound filled the cell, and the soldier staggered.

Sabin got to his feet and advanced. Finley was stabbing at the Kantos with wild, desperate hits.

He took the arm from her, then swung. The Kantos soldier's head hit the floor.

Finley grimaced. "Ew."

Sabin cupped her face. "Are you hurt?"

She shook her head. "I remembered your lesson on the weak spots." She smiled. "I might've been a little distracted by my instructor, but I remembered something."

He pressed a quick kiss to her mouth. "We need to move."

She nodded, pushing her hair out of her face. "Now what?"

"Now, we're going to steal a swarm ship." It had been done before. "Let's go."

CHAPTER SIXTEEN

The Kantos battlecruiser was a horrible place.

Fear was a tight ball in Finley's gut. The ship smelled bad. Like dog poop warmed up and mixed with week-old, rotten trash. She heard strange, distant noises. She stayed close to Sabin as they jogged down the corridor. The brown walls looked like an insect shell, and glowed in places with an eerie, gold light

Sabin was limping. Her heart lurched. He was really hurt and had to be in a lot of pain.

Suddenly, he staggered.

"*Sabin.*" She grabbed him, and leaned his weight against the wall. His breathing was raspy.

"Just... Need a minute."

"We need to get your helian free."

"There is an antidote." A faint smile crossed his lips. "I don't have it with me. Come on, we can't stop."

She kept her arm around him. God, he was heavy. That he put so much weight on her told her how badly he was hurt.

She heard the beat of Kantos footsteps approaching—the sharp clip of claws on the floor.

Pulse leaping, Finley pushed Sabin into a shadowed alcove. They pressed against the wall.

Please don't see us.

Several Kantos soldiers marched past in an adjoining corridor.

Once they were gone, she blew out a breath.

"Come on, Sabin." She helped him get moving. How the hell was he going to fly a ship?

They moved into a larger corridor. There were several doorways lining one side, and she glanced through one. Inside, the walls were covered with large, cocoon-like pods, and she shivered at the sight.

All of a sudden, a bug skidded into view. It was a little bigger than a dog, with a yellow carapace. It was delicate, with six skinny legs and a flat face. Two large, black eyes looked at them.

As far as bugs went, it was actually kind of cute.

"What is it?" she whispered.

"I've never seen it before."

A fan-like set of antennae rose up on its head. It almost looked like feathers. The antenna started out yellow near the head and changed colors to a vibrant purple at the top. The fans waved hypnotically. Well. It was the first time she'd seen a pretty Kantos.

"Hey." Sabin shook her. "Don't look at the antenna."

"What?"

"You froze, like you were in a trance."

Oh, hell. Maybe it wasn't so pretty after all. The creature shifted closer, then spat a ball of something at them.

Sabin slammed into Finley, knocking her out of the way. The poison hit the wall and started chewing a hole in it.

"*Cren*. It hypnotizes, and then poisons."

"Wonderful," she bit out.

The Kantos bug moved closer.

"I need to take it down. Stay back."

She grabbed his arm. "Sabin, you're hurt. You can't do this alone."

A muscle in his jaw ticked.

"We'll do it together," she said.

"You're the bravest woman I know, Finley Delgado."

They turned.

"One," she said. "Two. *Three*."

They rushed the Kantos. Another ball of poison sprayed into the air, and Finley ducked. She slid in and crashed into the alien. She slammed into its legs, and it let out a low screech.

Sabin leaped on top of it. He grabbed the fan-like antennae and snapped them off.

The Kantos bug made a horrible noise, then curled in on itself.

Finley rolled away. The Kantos was in a tight ball and not moving. Sabin was on his hands and knees, breathing hard.

"Sabin." She crawled to him and touched his back.

"I'm...okay."

There was so much pain in his voice. Tears pricked her eyes.

"Come on," he said.

The man never gave up. She helped him to his feet.

They hobbled along until they reached a junction. A buzzing noise filled the air. Finley peered carefully around a corner, gasped, and jerked back.

Sabin watched her, his eyes hooded. "What is it?"

Despair pulled at her. "More of those yellow creatures. I'd guess about thirty of them. They're blocking the corridor."

Sabin cursed. "Cutting us off from the main hangar."

And the swarm ships.

"Now what?" she asked.

"Plan B," Sabin said.

"What's Plan B?"

He grabbed her hand and pulled her in the opposite direction. "I'm not sure yet."

"What?"

"Just don't stop."

They jogged down the hall. She kept glancing at him. His face was so pale, and he was sweating profusely.

"Stop here." She pulled them to a halt. "Are you okay?"

That muscle ticked in his jaw again. "Yes."

"Liar."

"I won't stop until you're safe."

The words and the look in his eyes melted her. He would do exactly what he promised. He was the most honest, honorable man she knew. She felt a flash of emotion under her heart. She was falling in love with Sabin.

This day was officially the craziest day ever.

She heard the Kantos in the corridor getting closer.

"Come on." He grabbed her hand.

They started moving the other way. He yanked her down another corridor.

He was slowing down, his limp worsening. "Sabin?"

"I have some internal bleeding."

No. Brent had died of his internal bleeding. Old, ugly memories crashed in on her like a swarm of locust.

No. She couldn't lose it. She had to stay strong and help Sabin. She *couldn't* lose Sabin.

Suddenly, he stopped. "Here."

A door was set into the wall in front of them. Sabin tapped the wall and yanked open a panel. Wires, organic looking tubes, and some brown ooze filled the small compartment.

He did something inside the compartment, and the larger door slid open. Inside, was what looked like a large cocoon. The top half of it was open.

"What's that?" she asked.

"A Kantos escape pod. Get in."

She spun to look at him. "What?"

"We can't get to the swarm ships. I won't last much longer. I need you to get in. I'll program a signal that the *Rengard* can pick up. You'll be safe."

Her eyes widened. "You're coming, too."

"I need to keep the Kantos distracted so they don't realize the pod's gone."

"*No.*" She grabbed his arms. "I am *not* leaving without you."

His jaw tightened. "Finley—"

"No." She shook her head. "You and me, or I stay and help you fight."

He growled.

"I won't lose you," she whispered.

"*Cren.*" He yanked her in for a kiss. "Fine. Get in."

Her eyes narrowed. "You first."

He scowled and climbed into the cocoon pod. She climbed in beside him. It wasn't huge, and it was oddly shaped, but there was plenty of room for them.

The door closed, and red lights flickered to life.

"Buckle in the best you can. These are designed for Kantos bodies." He touched the controls.

Then, without any warning, a low beep sounded, and the pod jettisoned into space.

Finley was pushed back against the pod seat, and her stomach dropped. *Oh, God.*

SABIN WISHED he had control of his helian, so he could hack right into the escape pod controls.

Finley was clinging to him, but not panicking. That was his tough, gorgeous Terran.

He worked the controls and hoped the Kantos ship hadn't noticed them leave.

The pod jolted wildly.

"Oh, God, what's happening?" she asked.

Sabin squeezed her arm. "The battlecruiser's firing on us."

She made a sound and pressed her face to his chest. "Is there anything I can do to help?"

"No. I'll try to get us out of range."

He wished again for his helian. The pod wasn't very maneuverable. He checked the screen and saw that there was a large planet nearby, though he wasn't sure what it was. He did a brief scan and was grateful that the atmosphere was reading in range for him and Finley to be able to breathe. The air might be a little thin, but it was fine.

"Can you send a signal to your warship?"

"No. The Kantos would target us."

Her nose wrinkled. "You said you'd send one if you sent me out in the pod."

"Yes. Because I would have provided enough distraction to keep them off you. If I send one now, it will just help them hone in on us."

Suddenly, the pod was clipped by laser fire, and they spun out of control.

Finley screamed.

Sabin gritted his teeth and fought for control. "The pod's systems are damaged." More laser fire winged past them, making the pod rock. "We're losing oxygen."

"Sabin..."

He met her gaze. "I'm *not* going to let you die. We're heading for the planet."

She nodded. "I trust you. Whatever happens...I'm glad we're together."

He quickly kissed her.

The controls made a squawking sound. "We're entering the planet's atmosphere."

The ride got bumpy, the pod spinning and jerking.

He wrapped his arm around Finley. He looked at the screen and took a deep breath.

"Brace for impact."

"Sabin—"

He pulled her closer and kissed her.

They hit the ground with a bone-jarring impact. They were tossed around, the pod tipping over and over and over.

Finley cried out.

He held her tightly as they slid along the ground and finally stopped.

By Ston's sword, he *never* wanted to do that again.

"Finley?"

"I never want to go into space again," she said.

Her tone was a little shaky, and he pressed a kiss to the top of her head. "Are you injured?"

"A few bumps, but I'm fine." She looked at him. "You?"

His body was a mass of agony. "I'm fine."

"Liar."

"Let's get out of here. The Kantos will come searching."

He touched the controls, and the pod opened with a hiss. Sunlight flowed over them, combined with an eerie silence.

They climbed out of the pod and he stifled a groan. Finley helped him stand.

"The oxygen's a little low," he warned her, "so take it easy."

She nodded, looking around. They were standing in the center of a city, nestled in a valley between several hills. It was abandoned, with recent signs of fighting.

All the buildings gleamed, made from a white stone, but many were marred with scorch marks. Some of them were just rubble. All around them, the trees had been stripped of leaves, and there wasn't much greenery left.

"What happened here?" Finley murmured.

Sabin shook his head. He had a suspicion of where they were.

Finley wandered down the cobblestone street. On the mountain top above them sat a ruined temple. The design was elegant, even beautiful. The ruined city's architecture was artful, with lots of quiet pools and now-still fountains.

There were also several overturned transports in the street.

Finley gasped.

"What?" He hurried to her.

"God." Tears shimmered in her eyes and she pressed her hand to her mouth. "Sabin, look."

The street was littered with desiccated skeletons. They were humanoid.

"Where are the animals? There are no birds, no insects." Her eyes widened. "The Kantos attacked here." Horror filled her eyes.

He sighed. "I suspect this is the planet C'addon. The Kantos recently attacked it."

"Everyone's dead. Wiped out like they never existed." She swallowed, then her eyes sparked. "I'm not letting them do this to Earth."

Sabin hugged her. "Right now, we need to focus on calling for help."

There was a rush of sound in the sky. They both turned and saw several swarm ships in the distance.

Cren. Sabin hurried back to the pod and pulled some rubble over it. "Come on."

They jogged toward the closest buildings and ducked inside. They hunkered down, just as a swarm ship swept right overhead.

Finley stifled a gasp as the ship kicked dust up.

"They're searching for us," she said.

"Yes." He scanned the ruined city and then glanced up again at the temple on the hill. "We need to set off my emergency beacon signal for the *Rengard*." The Kantos would intercept it, so he and Finley would need to evade them until the *Rengard* arrived. "The temple is the highest point. We'll climb up there, and I'll activate the beacon."

She nodded, her face set. "Let's do it."

Once the swarm ship had moved into the distance, they darted out.

"Look," she said.

She pointed at stairs cut into the cliff face, leading to the temple. They hurried closer.

"I hear a swarm ship," he said.

There was a ruined stone archway nearby. They ducked down, just as the ship roared overhead. He saw it land several streets away.

Cren.

"Stay low." Hunched over, they ran toward the stairs.

There was a buzzing sound in the air, and he knew that Kantos soldiers were close.

Finley's eyes went wide.

He pulled her behind a transport. It was abandoned, with the door open like a person had just left it.

He pressed his fingers to his lips.

There was a crunching sound. He glanced through the transport windows and saw two Kantos soldiers step into view. He stiffened.

Something touched his boot and he looked down to see a bright-green lizard. It licked his boot, then looked up at him with huge, dark eyes.

He nudged it to go away, and it froze. Its legs were sticking out and its skin changed color to blend in with the transport.

Finley made a sound, and he realized that she was trying not to laugh. The creature had frozen with its leg stuck in the air, so it didn't blend in very well.

The small thing did look pretty comical.

The creature glanced at Finley, and it changed to a pink color.

Then they heard the Kantos getting closer, and the lizard dived into Finley's lap.

CHAPTER SEVENTEEN

Finley held her breath. The Kantos soldiers were *right* on the other side of the archway.

The little lizard quivered. She stroked it. It seemed friendly, and it was a cute little thing.

"They're gone." Sabin rose and pulled her up with him.

The lizard scrambled up and perched on her shoulder.

They hurried over to the stairs, and started up the stone-cut steps.

Oh, man. Soon she was huffing and puffing, her lungs burning.

Sabin was perspiring. He didn't complain, but his face was swollen, and horrible bruises were forming. She wished they could figure out a way to free his helian.

"I need...a rest," she said. Really, she wanted him to rest.

He nodded and they stopped in a small alcove cut into the rock. There was a carved bench seat there. She imagined that pilgrims heading up to the temple used the spot to rest.

They had an excellent view of the city. It must have been beautiful before its destruction. There were so many fountains, pools of water, and narrow channels joining them. It must have been amazing when the fountains and pools were running.

"It looks pretty from up here."

"The C'addonites were known for their temples, rituals, and festivals to worship their goddesses."

"Those poor people."

Sabin leaned heavily against the rock wall. Finley rose and went to him. "How are you doing?"

He gave a curt nod.

She touched him, hating that he was in pain.

"Your friend likes you," he said.

The lizard darted out from her hair. It was now yellow with blue stripes.

"If only he could fight off the Kantos," she said.

"Let's keep climbing."

After that, it became one foot in front of the other. Finley's thigh muscles burned. She glanced down. The city lay far below. Movement caught her eye on the ground, and she realized it was Kantos patrols.

Searching for them.

They kept moving upward and finally crested the top of the stairs.

"No more stairs." *Yay.*

Ahead lay the spire of the temple. The main body of the temple was ruined. It looked like it had been hit by laser fire. What was left of the white-stone walls was covered with scorch marks.

The people who'd lived here didn't deserve this. Earth didn't deserve this.

Sabin pulled out a small device that was hidden under his armor. It looked like a large coin, with a blue light on top.

"Let's get the beacon activated," he said.

They moved inside the part of the temple that was still standing. It was quiet and shadowed, and more skeletons lay inside, resting against the wall.

Her heart clenched. *Rest in peace.*

They moved up some circular stairs, heading up to the top of the spire.

When they reached the top, the wind tugged at Finley's hair and her lizard friend buried himself against her neck. Sabin pressed the beacon against the rock wall and pressed something on the device to activate it.

Beep.

"Now we need to hide." He frowned. "The Kantos will track the signal and come after us."

They hurried back down the stairs and headed back toward the rock-cut steps. But she heard noises down below and gasped.

Kantos soldiers were racing up the stone steps.

Sabin cursed. "There must be other paths."

They headed back past the temple, circling a sunken pool and fountain.

"There." She pointed at another path leading down to the city.

Suddenly, Finley heard a flap of sound in the air. A

Kantos assassin landed between them and the second set of stairs.

She stepped back. Another assassin landed behind them.

Shit.

The lizard on her shoulder froze.

Sabin attacked the first assassin. The pair whirled and kicked at each other.

But she could see Sabin was slower than usual, his injuries zapping his energy. The assassin landed a hard kick, and Sabin staggered backward.

No.

"I'll keep him busy," he yelled. "Get to the stairs."

"I'm not leaving you!"

The other assassin screeched.

"Your life means everything to me," Sabin said. "*Please.*"

The air whooshed out of her. "Sabin." She couldn't leave him behind.

"Get to the stairs!"

He was planning to sacrifice himself for her.

"No." She crouched and grabbed a hunk of rock from the rubble.

Sabin growled. "Stubborn Terran."

"Yes, but I'm *your* stubborn Terran."

One of the assassins attacked him.

Finley turned to face the second one.

It advanced on her, its wings outstretched.

She ignored her fear. It flew at her, and she whacked it with the rock. Her lizard friend darted onto her back. She hit the Kantos assassin again.

She felt claws rake her spacesuit, but the fabric protected her. She hit it again.

Suddenly, the assassin flew into the air, hovering. She threw the rock.

It hit the creature's wing, hitting a small bone. She heard it snap. With a screech, it crashed over the side of the cliff.

"Yes! Sabin—" She spun and froze.

He was collapsed on the ground, not moving. The other assassin was nearby, ready and waiting.

Her chest locked. "Sabin? Sabin, get up!"

He didn't move.

The assassin advanced.

Finley lifted her chin. Then with a cry, she charged. She was so damn tired of being afraid. She lowered her head and tackled the assassin, and they hit the dirt together.

"Why won't you just leave us alone?" She smacked her elbow into its head. "I *won't* be your damn prey anymore."

It threw her off and rose into the air.

She hit the ground with an *oof* and rolled. She almost fell into a sunken pool nearby.

She turned, and saw the assassin looking at the spire.

It must be searching for the beacon. *No, you don't, asshole.*

"Look over here, you ugly bug."

Those multifaceted eyes turned her way.

"I'm going to find a way to kill you," Finley said.

It let out a screech.

"But first, you get away from my man."

The assassin flew at her. She ducked, and one of its claws tangled in her hair.

Ow. She pulled free, tearing hair loose as she did.

She had to get to Sabin.

"Sabin." She slid to her knees beside him. "*Sabin.*"

He groaned. He was alive, thank God.

She gripped his shoulder. "We have a Kantos assassin to kill, and soldiers incoming."

He pushed up onto his knees. He was so shaky, his face ghost white.

The assassin hovered nearby, watching them steadily.

"You get to the stairs," Sabin ground out.

"No."

He shook his head. "Despite your stubbornness, I'm falling in love with you, Finley."

Oh, God. "Sabin..." Her chest was tight; she couldn't breathe.

She helped him up and together they faced the assassin.

"I will keep you safe." He squeezed her hand. "It's my duty, my honor." Jaw tight, Sabin rushed toward the assassin.

No. Finley sucked in a breath. He launched himself at the alien.

He launched up, grabbed the assassin's scaly feet and yanked it to the ground. Then assassin and warrior attacked each other.

It was a vicious fight, both of them taking blows.

Finley bit her lip. She had to find a way to help him.

Then Sabin leaped onto the assassin. He gripped its flapping wings.

His gaze met hers. "Be safe, Finley. Be strong."

With a hard shove, he knocked the assassin off its feet. Together, they fell over the cliff edge. Sabin dropped, taking the assassin with him. He kept its wings from flaring out.

No! Finley couldn't breathe. She stared at the empty space where Sabin had been. The lizard turned in agitated circles on her shoulder. She raced to the edge and looked down.

The assassin and Sabin lay crumpled on the ground below.

So far down.

Tears welled in her eyes and her throat closed.

"*Sabin.*" She ran for the stairs.

SABIN COULDN'T MOVE.

With a groan, he lifted his head. His body was a massive throb of agony. He was lying on a flat, stone area ringed by fountains and narrow channels of water.

He was bleeding; he smelled it, felt it. The life was flowing out of him.

He rolled and bit back a groan. He panted through the pain as his vision swam. He sucked in air. His legs wouldn't move.

Where was Finley? She had to be okay. The *Rengard* would come, and she'd be safe.

He heard a low noise and glanced over. The crumpled assassin lay nearby, its legs and wings broken from the fall.

Painfully, Sabin dragged himself closer. The assassin saw him, and tried to slash out with its claws.

Sabin grabbed the Kantos and wrestled it. He felt claws rake his side. He got the assassin in a chokehold and then pulled back with all his strength.

As the Kantos died, it thrashed, but Sabin held on.

Then the alien slumped.

Panting, Sabin rolled onto his back. His gaze was blurry, but he could make out the blue sky and the spire on the mountain above.

Then he heard running footsteps.

Finley's face appeared in front of his.

"*God.* Sabin." She cupped his face.

He saw the lizard, now a brilliant purple, dart across her shoulders.

Her face twisted. "Don't move."

He drew in a breath and heard it rattle. "Fin-ley."

She bit her lip, tears running down her cheeks. "You're going to be okay."

They both knew that was a lie. He was dying. He could feel his body shutting down.

"Love...you."

She closed her eyes and leaned over him, pressing her forehead to his. "I love you, too. I'm *not* going to let you leave me. You think I'm perfect. You love me. I need you, Sabin."

The lizard leaped onto his chest and they ignored it.

"You're...strong," he said.

"Please, Sabin."

There was noise nearby and her head jerked up.

The lizard squeaked and dived into Finley's hair.

"Finley?" Sabin said.

The color drained from her face. "Bugs. A whole group of them." She swallowed. "They're smallish, cat-sized, with sharp teeth."

Sabin howled inside. He couldn't protect her. He tried to sit up.

"No." She pressed a hand to his chest. She followed it with a light kiss. "I'm going to protect *you*, this time."

He could see she was afraid, but she was trying to hide it.

"Smart," he said. "Use...that brain of yours."

FINLEY TRIED NOT TO PANIC. Seeing Sabin so hurt was bad enough, but seeing those bugs coming was really bad.

"Think, Finley, think."

Her lizard friend was agitated, and it leaped to the ground. He moved to the first channel of water, squeaked, and darted back toward her. It was very agitated. Next, it moved over to a fountain. It made frantic moves again and Finley shifted closer. She smelled something.

She knelt, one eye on the hovering bugs. The water had a shimmering gleam to it.

She frowned and touched it. It was sticky. She sniffed it.

It wasn't water. It was some sort of oil. She looked at the connected fountains and channels. They were all filled with oil.

Her thoughts turned. The fountains and channels snaked all around. Sabin was lying in the center of a circular channel.

Bugs hated fire.

She spun. Damn, she had no way to light the oil. The bugs moved closer, and now, she heard a buzzing in the air. She glanced over and saw Kantos soldiers coming closer, as well.

Every muscle in her stomach tied into knots.

Sabin groaned. Dammit, she would protect the man she loved.

She saw some rocks that had clearly fallen from the cliff. She snatched up two of them. She'd fight for the people who'd died here, as well as for her and Sabin's survival.

"You will not be forgotten," she whispered furiously.

She grabbed the rocks and leaned over the oil. She struck them together.

Nothing happened.

She kept trying. Crap, this always seemed easy in the movies.

The lizard darted closer, its big eyes wide. It was changing colors rapidly, obviously afraid.

A bug moved closer, on the opposite side of one of the oil channels. It was watching them carefully.

Tears of frustration filled Finley's eyes. "Come *on*."

She did a huge strike and the tiniest spark flared before it was gone. She hadn't gotten it anywhere near the oil.

This wasn't going to work.

Her shoulders slumped and a tear rolled down her cheek.

She'd failed again.

She wasn't perfect, or clever, or brave. Sabin would pay the price, like Brent and Melody had.

"I'm sorry," she said.

Sabin's face was turned toward her. He held out a hand, his face twisted into a grimace. She saw that there was blood under him, smeared on the stone.

She wanted to crawl to him and hold him tight.

She tried striking the rocks again.

The lizard cocked its head, watching.

She managed another tiny spark and gasped. But it petered out as well, and the bugs were getting very close now.

"No, *dammit*," she cried.

The lizard moved closer and its skin turned red. Then it turned his head and opened his mouth.

Flames shot out.

Holy cow. She jerked backward and fell on her ass.

"Little guy, do that again." She scrambled up. "On the oil."

Like he knew exactly what she was saying, the lizard moved closer to the oil and let out a stream of flames.

The oil ignited.

Mouth dropping open, she watched as the fire ran along the channel and then through the fountains. The fountains turned into springs of cascading fire. The channels turned into a wall of flame, rising high, circling around her and Sabin.

CHAPTER EIGHTEEN

S abin stared at the flames then turned to look at Finley. She grabbed the small lizard, and held it to her face. It nuzzled her cheek.

"Thank you. Thank you!"

Through the flames, he saw the Kantos bugs had stopped, staring at them hungrily.

Sabin tried to focus. "Well done, Dr. Delgado."

She dropped down beside him, her fingers brushing his cheek. "I had a little help."

"I saw that."

The lizard ran along her arm. She glanced at the flames and bit her lip. "I'm not sure the fire will hold them for long."

He grunted. Nothing stopped the Kantos for long. He pulled in a breath, but it was hard. He was weak and it was hard to keep his eyes open.

"Sabin, no. Stay awake." Her voice was laced with desperation. "Stay with me."

He reached out and managed to grab her hand. "I love you, Finley. Everything about you."

"I know you didn't want to fall in love. That you were afraid."

"I was so wrong. So scared." He smiled. "Not anymore. You make me stronger, more centered."

She lowered her head and pressed her mouth to his.

Then he grimaced.

"Sabin? God, there's so much blood."

"Finley, I'm going soon." He felt it. His energy draining.

"*No.*" She shook her head. "No, no, no."

The lizard ran along his arm, now a deep black color, like he'd picked up her sorrow.

She pressed her forehead to Sabin's. "I don't want to lose you."

"Hurts." His voice was losing strength.

She swallowed a cry. "I don't want you hurting."

All of a sudden, Sabin felt a flicker from his helian. He sucked in a breath.

"Sabin?" Her fingers tightened on him.

"I felt my helian."

Her eyes widened and she looked down. "Oh, my God. The lizard is eating the goo on your helian band."

Sabin turned his head and saw the little creature licking at his helian band, black around its mouth. It kept munching.

"God," Finley breathed.

Sabin felt his helian breaking through, starting to take over. His body arched.

"Sabin?"

"My helian is...healing me." But it hurt. His symbiont was pouring everything it had into healing his injuries. Energy filled him.

"Thank God." Finley wiped her tears away and smiled.

"Help me up."

With Finley's help, Sabin rose. He was still shaky, and he knew it would take a while to heal all his wounds.

The lizard leaped on his shoulder. "Thanks, little guy."

It squeaked and froze with its leg sticking out again.

Sabin turned his head and looked through the flames. He stiffened.

Kantos soldiers and bugs were pacing. Getting ready to attack.

"Finley, behind me."

As they turned, he saw that there was an entire circle of Kantos surrounding them, just outside the flames.

Cren. It would be impossible to keep her safe.

Where the hell were Malax and Airen? He scanned the sky, but all he saw were the shadows of two moons, and no *Rengard.*

He commanded his helian to form his sword, and the long, black blade extended.

"Sabin, you're in no condition to fight. You aren't healed yet."

He gripped her chin. "I don't have a choice. The Kantos are about to attack."

Fear flared, but she lifted her chin. "We're not giving up."

"We're not giving up," he echoed. "I can..."

"What?" She gripped his arm.

"I can let my senses free."

She sucked in a breath. "What do you mean?"

"The full spectrum of my enhanced abilities will let me sense things quicker, move faster."

"It'll help you! Do it."

A muscle ticked in his jaw. "But if I lose total control—"

"You won't." She rose up and kissed him. "You're my strong, disciplined, honorable warrior." She smiled. "I know you can do this."

A hunting bug leaped through the fire.

Sabin stepped forward and threw the chains off his senses. He'd do anything to keep Finley safe.

Everything expanded—his eyesight, his smell, his hearing, his touch. Sensation and energy flooded his body.

The bug attacked and he knew exactly where it was aiming. He could read every move a fraction of a second before it happened. He slashed out with his sword. He kicked the bleeding bug back into the flames.

It screeched and struggled as it burned.

Another one leaped through. Then another.

Sabin fought, his senses open wide, his focus on nothing but the swing of his sword.

Then he heard Finley cry out.

He swiveled, his heart thumping.

Three bugs were advancing on her from the other side of the circle.

One jumped, and suddenly the lizard ran along her

arm and opened its mouth. It breathed fire in the face of the bug.

The Kantos crashed to the ground, shaking its burning head.

Sabin slashed at a second bug. A third one leaped at Finley. They crashed to the ground, the bug on top of her.

"Finley!" Sabin growled.

He took two steps to help her when a soldier dove through the wall of fire. It attacked him and he whipped his sword up.

He saw Finley struggling to push the bug off her, its snapping mandibles getting closer and closer to her face.

She had no weapon. No way to defend herself.

His heart was beating like a drum in his chest. "Finley!"

Suddenly, scales flew off Sabin's armor, moving through the air like a black cloud.

They hit Finley's body, flowing over her.

With a screech, the bug leaped off her.

Sabin's heart stopped.

Finley rose, staring at her body.

Finley was his mate.

A sense of rightness filled him. Of course, she was. "Finley, think of a shield and a weapon."

She held out her arms. The black-scale armor covered her snugly. Suddenly, a glowing purple energy shield formed on her left arm and a short sword on her right.

"I can't use a sword," she cried.

The Kantos soldier attacked Sabin again and he

looked away from her. He kicked and slashed at his opponent.

"Just swing it," he yelled over his shoulder.

A bug attacked her. She held up the shield and drove the bug back. She jabbed with the sword.

She clipped the bug and sent it through the fire.

Sabin kept fighting the soldier, working his way toward her. His happiness at seeing her safe in his armor bled away.

"There are so many," she breathed.

The lizard peeked out of her hair.

Kantos soldiers and bugs filled the streets of the ruined city. They were all converging on Sabin and Finley.

Sabin pulled her close. They couldn't lose hope.

"Stay strong, my gorgeous mate."

"Mate?" She shook her head. "This has been a hell of a day. My first trip to space, my first spacewalk, my first— and I hope only—abduction by aliens, my first time on an alien planet, and now mated to a sexy alien warrior."

Two soldiers leaped through the fire on the far side of the circle.

"Let's fight, mate of mine." Sabin charged.

Finley was right behind him.

They kicked and slashed and skewered. Finley fought —she wasn't skilled, but she was fueled by the will to survive.

But as they fought the Kantos, he knew that they were both tiring. His body was still healing his injuries, and several had started bleeding again.

A soldier rammed into him from the side and he fell to his knees.

"Sabin!" Finley fought to get to him.

An elite emerged from the flames. *Time to die, Eon.*

Suddenly, a body swooped in and landed in a crouch in front of Sabin. For a second, he thought it was a Kantos assassin.

But the figure rose, a powerful body covered in black-scale armor, with wings that retracted back into the armor.

War Commander Malax Dann-Jad.

More bodies landed. Airen. Donovan. The warriors of Sabin's security team.

They all formed long swords and attacked.

THANK. *God.*

Finley watched the Eon warriors fight, relief punching through her. She kicked a bug and held her shield up to block another one.

Nearby, an Eon shuttle, followed by several sleek Eon fighters, whizzed past, opening fire on Kantos in the streets.

She worked her way back to Sabin. He was already looking stronger, standing taller. Her lizard friend curled around her ear.

Sabin saw her, emotion filling his face. He yanked her into his arms as the fight raged around them. His arms were so tight she could barely breathe.

"Sabin."

His hold loosened.

She cupped his cheeks. His eyes were flickering, his nostrils flared. "Are you all right?"

"*Cren.*" He pressed his face against her hair. "Yes. Sensory overload."

She kissed him, slowly, with deliberate gentleness. "Come back to me."

His hands flexed on her, then his eyes returned to normal. "Thank you, Finley."

"For what?" She clung to him. She never wanted to let him go.

"For not giving up." He met her gaze. "For saving me. For believing that I could control my senses."

"I'll never give up on you, and I trust you with everything I have."

They kissed.

She looked at the armor covering her. "So, we're mates."

"We are."

Her stomach did an uncomfortable roll. "You told me you never wanted a mate."

He had an unreadable look on his face. "I never—"

"Sabin." Malax strode to them. The man radiated authority and was a little intimidating.

"Malax." The men clasped arms in a warrior grasp.

Finley saw the other warriors had finished dispatching the Kantos. The rest had run and were being chased down by Eon fighter ships.

The warriors moved closer. She noted that one man—with dark skin and a muscular body—was actually human. She realized it was Sub-Captain Donovan

Lennox. The Space Corps officer was assigned to the *Rengard*, and mated to the tough female warrior, Airen Kann-Felis, the second commander of the *Rengard*. Finley guessed it was the tall, sleek woman standing beside him.

Sabin greeted the warriors. "I'm glad you weren't any later."

"We met a little resistance getting here." Airen's gaze flicked to Finley in her scale armor, then back to Sabin. "I see you've been busy."

"Sabin, I'm afraid this isn't over." Malax's face was deadly serious, and Finley's stomach dropped.

Sabin slid an arm across her shoulders. "Tell us."

Malax paused. "Congratulations on your mating."

Sabin didn't respond. God, was he even happy about it? He'd told her that he loved her, but she knew that he'd never wanted to mate.

"The Kantos fleet is about to attack Earth," Malax said.

Finley gasped. "The StarStorm?"

"Space Corps is trying to get it operational, but they need your expertise, Dr. Delgado."

"Let's go."

A shuttle landed nearby and as they moved toward it, the little lizard, now vibrant green, turned around on her palm. "You're safe now, little guy."

She lowered her hand and the lizard leaped off. It squeaked, then moved over to touch her hand—like a kiss —then with one last look, it darted away.

"Good luck." Sadness moved through her, but hope, as well. Hope that her little friend would thrive, and that this world would recover. She scanned the ruins and prayed that somewhere, some of its residents remained hidden and safe.

Now, she had to save Earth.

The Eon shuttle was sleek and spacious. Much nicer than Space Corps' designs. Within minutes, they were strapped into plush seats and zooming away from C'addon.

Finley bounced her leg, nerves getting the better of her.

"Hey." Sabin's hand rested on her thigh. "It's going to be fine."

She nodded.

A warrior sat beside them. "Glad to see that you're still alive."

He had gray threaded through his brown hair, although he didn't look much older than Sabin.

With a smile, Sabin gave the man a one-armed hug, slapping his back. "Finley, this is Medical Commander Thane Kann-Eon."

"I'm this guy's closest friend, and medical commander of the *Rengard*." Thane's green-black gaze took in Finley's armor and his eyes widened. "You're mated." He grinned.

"So it seems," Sabin said.

Again, Finley's nerves jittered. That wasn't a ringing endorsement. She clutched her hands together.

"You're looking a little battered, Sabin," Thane said.

"Been a bit of a rough day."

The doctor pulled out a vial of *havv* and something

inside of Finley eased. Finally, she knew Sabin would be okay. Fully healed.

She sat quietly as Thane administered the *havv*.

"We'll be docking soon," a warrior called out.

She looked out the side window and saw the *Rengard*.

The warship was impressive. It was obvious Eon tech was way ahead of Earth's. She remembered how disdainful she'd been of Sabin when she'd first met him, and shook her head.

A large door opened in the black hull of the warship, and the shuttle entered the docking bay. Once they'd set down, Sabin led her off the shuttle. More of Sabin's team met him, clasping arms with him.

"We need to get to the bridge," Malax said.

Sabin moved to Finley. She was feeling awkward and out of place. It was clear Sabin belonged here, and was well-respected.

And her place was back in her lab on Earth.

Her throat tightened and she followed the war commander. A second later, Sabin was with her, taking her arm.

"Are you all right?" he asked.

She nodded. "Just worried."

He touched her hair. "Let's go kick some Kantos ass."

She smiled. "Who taught you that expression?"

"Gemma."

"I think Earth has corrupted you."

"Maybe." He smiled back.

They moved through the sleek, black corridors of the

Rengard. There were more warriors in black uniforms. The entire place was awe-inspiring.

Then they stepped onto the bridge.

Wow. There were several tiers of workstations, with busy warriors behind them. A huge viewscreen dominated the space.

"Prep us to jump," Malax ordered.

"Finley!"

She turned and saw Wren Traynor. "Wren."

The woman hurried over and hugged Finley.

Finley felt a prick of tears and hugged the woman back.

"You're okay?" Wren glanced over her, and saw the Eon armor. "You're mated? Oh my God, Sabin." Wren spun and hugged the warrior as well.

"Wren, we don't have time." Malax put his hand on his mate's shoulder. "We need to get to Earth."

"Let's go, then."

Finley listened to the war commander give orders. Sabin held her hand.

"It won't take long."

The jump to light speed initiated, and there was a second of disorientation. Warriors shouted orders. They did another jump, and another.

Finley's head was spinning.

Jarringly, Earth appeared on screen. Alarms screeched.

"Kantos fleet in range," Airen yelled.

Another screen showed the incoming fleet of Kantos ships.

No. Finley's mouth dropped open. There were so many.

Sabin moved to a light table, swiping its surface, a frown appearing on his face. One of his warriors moved up beside him, asking questions.

He belonged here. That was clear.

"Finley, Dr. Gregson and Admiral Barber for you," Donovan called out.

She turned and on a different screen, she saw the faces of the admiral and head scientist.

"Thank God you're both okay," the admiral said.

"It was touch and go," Finley said.

"Finley, we've replaced the destroyed satellite, but there is still some problem in the programming. We can't get the StarStorm fully operational."

Oh, God.

"I need access to the StarStorm system," Finley said. "Now!"

"Here." Sabin pointed to the light table. She saw her code appear on the screen and swiped.

"You have three minutes until the lead Kantos ship is in range," Airen said.

Finley's chest locked. That wasn't enough time. Her head wasn't in the right place. She needed calm. She needed to be in her lab. She needed—

Then there was a touch on her back. She looked at Sabin. Everything zeroed down to the two of them.

"Do what you do best, my smart Terran."

She nodded and swiped at the screen. She stared at the lines of code filling the table. She touched and swiped, losing herself in the data and the numbers.

There. She found the issue. And the targeting needed another tweak.

"One minute until the Kantos are in range," a warrior called out.

"Lead battlecruiser is spooling weapons," Airen said.

Finley blocked it out. She added in the correct code.

"Fire on the Kantos ship," Malax ordered.

"With pleasure," Sabin replied.

Finley kept working. She felt the *Rengard* shudder beneath her, and dimly heard the security team firing on the Kantos ships.

She looked up and saw the screen filled with arcs of laser fire.

"War Commander, the *Valantis* just arrived," someone called out.

On screen, another Eon warship appeared, firing on the Kantos.

"Sir, a Kantos battlecruiser just broke through. They're preparing to fire on Earth."

Finley put in the last bit of code. Everything clicked and went green on screen.

"I've got it!" she cried.

"Activate the StarStorm, Admiral," Malax yelled.

"Activating."

The seconds slowed and Finley stared at the screen. Sabin appeared by her side and took her hand.

They waited.

Come on.

She saw the battlecruiser getting closer and closer to the planet.

God, what if it didn't work?

The StarStorm lasers fired. The net started forming around Earth.

"My God," she breathed.

"You did it," Sabin said.

A shiny silver net of laser surrounded the planet.

"We did!" She jumped on him and kissed him.

The Kantos fired, but it rebounded off the StarStorm net.

The lead Kantos ship was moving at high speed, and already too close. It hit the net and part of the ship disintegrated, explosions flaring.

Cheers erupted on the bridge of the *Rengard*.

CHAPTER NINETEEN

Sabin watched the *Rengard* and the *Valantis* open fire. The Kantos fleet turned and ran.

"They're retreating," Airen called out.

His beautiful, talented, hard-working mate had done it. With a cheer, he picked Finley up and swung her around.

She looked dazed. "It worked. The StarStorm repelled the Kantos."

"You just dealt a heavy blow to the Kantos' invasion plans." He kissed her.

She kissed him back—a little wild, with an edge of desperation.

He frowned. *Something wasn't right.* "Finley?"

Then they were mobbed by the others.

"Finley, congrats!" Wren hugged her.

Malax, Airen, and Donovan slapped Sabin on the back.

But he kept one eye on Finley. She looked a little withdrawn.

Cren. Did she not want to be mated? That thought was like a rock in his gut.

No. She loved him. He felt in his bones that she was his. His helian pulsed.

"Well done, Sabin." Malax gripped his shoulder. "On the StarStorm, and on your mating."

Airen cocked her head. "You never wanted to mate."

His gaze fell on Finley. "I'd never give her up. She's everything."

"We'll talk later on how to make it work for you both," Malax said. "Now go, be with your mate."

Sabin strode across the bridge. "Can I steal my mate?"

Wren smiled at him. "Go. Finley, we'll catch up soon. We've got lots to talk about, including my tips on dealing with Eon warrior mates." She winked.

Finley smiled, but it didn't quite reach her eyes.

Frowning, Sabin pulled her off the bridge.

"You must have so much to do." She pushed her hair back behind her ears. "I can—"

He cupped her face. "Right now, all I want to focus on is my mate."

She licked her lips.

"Finley, talk to me. What's wrong?"

If she rejected that bond...

"You never wanted to mate." Her voice was hushed.

"It was your trust and encouragement that let me trust my abilities."

"And you have duties here, responsibilities—"

"I love you."

Her lips parted.

"Being with you has changed everything, and opened my eyes."

"Sabin—"

"It was fear that drove me not to want to mate." He smiled. "With you by my side, I'm not afraid of my extra senses." He lowered his voice. "I want to use them on you, every moment I can."

She blushed. "My work is on Earth, yours is here."

"We'll work it out. The Eon-Terran alliance isn't going anywhere, so there will be lots of opportunities. And to be with you, I'll do whatever I have to do."

"Oh, Sabin." Her face softened. "I love you so much."

He lifted her off her feet for a kiss. He pulled the taste of her in. He'd *never* get enough of her.

Suddenly, a cramp hit him. With a grunt, he set her down. Heat washed over his skin.

"Sabin? What's wrong? Are you hurt?"

"No." This was pure hunger. Hunger for his mate.

He closed in on her and backed her up. She gasped and her shoulder blades hit the wall.

His lips took hers. She melted against him and moaned into his mouth. When he lifted his head, his control was ragged.

"Sabin?" Her lips were swollen, a dazed look on her face.

"This is the mating fever."

"Oh?" She cupped his face. "I know you've dreaded it. Are you—?"

He grabbed her hand and pressed it to his pants, right over his straining cock.

She cupped him and bit her lip.

"I'm not afraid. I need you, Finley. So much."

"I'm yours."

Sabin scooped her into his arms and carried her down the corridor. He marched into a lift and hit the buttons.

Finally, they reached his cabin and he pressed a hand to the electronic lock.

He strode into his cabin and dropped her on his bed. He stood beside the bed, and his armor retracted. Finley's did as well. Then he tore off his uniform.

Her gaze was on him, inflaming his senses. He dropped his clothes on the floor.

"Take your clothes off, Finley."

Her gaze dropped to his straining cock. She lifted her chin. "*You* take my clothes off."

With a growl, he was on the bed, yanking her to the edge. A husky cry broke from her.

"This is going to be a little rough," he warned.

He reached out and opened the front fastening of her spacesuit, lowering it down over her breasts, her belly.

She shivered. "I'm okay with that."

"Rough and long." He pressed a kiss to her sternum. Her breasts quivered.

"How long?" she panted.

He tore her panties off, leaving his curvy mate naked.

"The mating fever usually lasts a few days."

Her eyes popped wide. "Days?"

He covered her body with his. "I promise you, you'll enjoy it."

Then he took her mouth with his and they were both lost.

SHE COULDN'T MOVE.

She would probably never move again.

Finley would just have to stay in Sabin's bed aboard the *Rengard,* forever.

She was on her belly and she languidly turned her head. Sabin was sleeping deeply beside her. She guessed they'd been locked in his cabin for about two days. She had vague memories of food being delivered, and his doctor friend Thane checking on them.

Sabin had been insatiable. Hell, *she'd* been insatiable. She made a contented sound.

It had been amazing. They'd made love every way they knew how. He'd shown her a few decadent new things, and she was pretty sure they'd invented a few others together.

She'd been totally wrong. Sex was the most amazing thing ever.

Finley shivered and moved closer to him. She pressed a kiss to his strong back.

She loved his body. She also loved his brain. She loved everything about this warrior. *Her* warrior.

They'd work this out. She knew they could.

He stirred, the muscles under her lips flexing. He rolled and then pulled her against his chest.

"How's my prickly *garva*?" He pressed a kiss to her hair.

"Alive, but my legs may never work again."

His hand skimmed down beside her thigh, and her leg twitched.

"It's a miracle," he said.

She smiled at him, taking in his body. He was fully healed. He'd proven that over the last couple of days.

"I suppose we should check in," she said.

Everyone would know exactly what they'd been doing. She tried not to feel embarrassed.

"Soon." He took her lips in a lazy kiss.

The door chimed. With a squeak, Finley dived under the covers.

"A friendly visit from the ship's doctor."

Thane entered, a smile on his face. The man was extremely attractive, and she fought her embarrassment.

"You've both eaten?" the doctor asked.

"We haven't wasted away." Sabin sat up.

"Good." Thane held up a handheld scanner. "Your biosigns are perfectly healthy. The mating fever's passed?"

Sabin nodded. He yanked Finley onto his lap. "We're great."

"Excellent. For a man who never wanted to mate, you look happy."

"I've never been happier," Sabin said.

Finley thought she saw a flash of pain in Thane's eyes, but then the doctor smiled at his friend. She looked at Sabin and happiness burst inside her. She knew he meant what he said. Being with him was one of the best things of her life. She wasn't sure what her family would think of her being mated to an Eon warrior, but if she was happy, they'd be happy, too.

"Well, I have a message for Finley," Thane said. "From a Gemma Neely and an Ian Cho. They've organized a celebration party at the Woomera Range Complex. All the *Rengard* crew are invited."

Sabin groaned. "Terrans need little excuse for a party."

"You both deserve a celebration. For the success of the StarStorm, for your mating, and for surviving the Kantos."

She met Sabin's eyes and they shared a smile. "A party might be nice."

Several hours later, Finley found herself aboard a packed shuttle heading back to Earth. Sabin sat beside her, Thane next to him. Wren and Malax were also aboard. Airen and Donovan had stayed on the *Rengard,* with a skeleton crew. There were several other shuttles full of warriors traveling to Earth as well.

She knew the Eon warriors were keen to see the planet they were helping to protect.

She was a little worried about how she and Sabin would make things work, but she had faith they would.

She pulled in a deep breath. She'd leave Earth if she had to. Surely there were some Eon research projects she could help with.

They landed at Woomera. As soon as she exited, Gemma and Ian rushed over for hugs.

"You're brilliant," Gemma exclaimed.

"Your help was invaluable in getting the StarStorm operational," Finley told her.

"Let's party!" Ian said.

Gemma tugged Finley away. "Party dresses are mandatory."

Finley groaned and shared a look with Sabin.

"I'll see you at the party," Sabin said.

Gemma dragged Finley down the hall. "You and Sabin are mated. You lucky woman."

Finley smiled. "We are. And I am."

"I might see if I can find myself a warrior." Gemma waggled her eyebrows.

Finley raised a brow. "Ian would be heartbroken."

The woman stumbled. "What?"

"He's totally head-over-heels for you."

"No," Gemma breathed. "We're just friends. Colleagues."

"Look more carefully, Gemma. You're a smart lady."

A speculative look crossed the young woman's face. "Maybe I will."

Soon they were dolled up, and Finley was wearing a little black dress. She found herself on the Woomera rooftop. Music was playing, and everyone was drinking and eating. Eon warriors mingled with Terrans.

Wren was dancing badly on a makeshift dance floor. She looked like she was having a seizure. Malax watched on, a smile on his face.

And love.

Finley searched for Sabin and spotted him talking with Kaira.

Finley headed over to them, and Kaira smiled at her.

"Welcome back and congratulations," the Woomera security commander said.

"Thank you," Finley replied.

"I'll let you have some time alone with your mate." With a smile, Kaira left them.

"Hi," Finley said.

"Hi. You look beautiful." Sabin pulled her into his arms. "We're right back where I first—"

"I remember." *Every second.*

"Look up."

Overhead was a bright sprinkle of stars.

"It's beautiful. Even more beautiful from down here, with my feet firmly on Earth."

"You helped save your planet, Finley. You saved me. In more ways than one."

She rubbed her nose against his. "And your steady belief and support led me here. We're a good team."

"And we'll be good mates."

Surrounded by Eon warriors and Terrans, they kissed under the stars.

CHAPTER TWENTY

Kaira

Kaira tried to relax.

It was a party, so there were lots of reasons to have fun.

She sighed. She was still acutely aware that there were Kantos out there. The StarStorm was a huge win, and would stop a large-scale attack.

But only when they saw the enemy coming.

It wouldn't stop small strike teams, or assassins sneaking through. She couldn't relax yet.

She glanced over and saw Finley in Sabin's arms. The scientist and the warrior were smiling at each other, and Kaira could practically feel the love from where she was standing.

Kaira was happy for them. A pang hit her under her heart. She'd had that once.

No, she wasn't going to have a pity party. She'd

grieved for Ryan, and would always miss him, but life marched on, whether you wanted it to or not.

She dated. She even caught up with a buddy with benefits occasionally, but she'd never let herself fall in love again.

It hurt too much to lose someone you loved. And she'd worked too hard putting the pieces of her life back together to have them shattered for a second time.

The doors to the roof opened, and two couples stepped onto the roof terrace.

"Eve! Lara!" Wren ran for the women.

Both of them were tall and athletic. The taller one was Lara Traynor. The one with a small, round pregnant belly would be Eve.

Wow, these women were Space Corps legends.

Kaira watched the three sisters embrace. The big warriors with them would be War Commander Davion Thann-Eon, and Security Commander Caze Vann-Jad of the *Desteron*.

Kaira wanted to meet the women. She had to admit she had a small girl crush on them both.

She grabbed a drink from the bar table and sipped. As she scanned the party again, her gaze snagged on a sexy, silver fox of an Eon warrior.

The man was talking with Sabin and Finley, so she guessed he was off the *Rengard*. *Yum*. Kaira felt a tingle. It'd been a long time since she'd felt much for a man. She drank him in. He'd be good fantasy material for when she was busy with her vibrator later.

Dragging her gaze off him, she noted when Lara and Eve were alone. She took her chance.

"Sub-Captain Traynor, Lieutenant Traynor. I'm Commander Kaira Chand, head of Woomera Security. It's an honor to meet you both."

"Likewise." Eve held out a hand while the other one rested on her belly. "And it's Ambassador Thann-Eon these days." The woman winced. "Although it's a hell of a mouthful."

"I heard you did good work here, Commander Chand," Lara said. "You helped fight off the Kantos."

"We desperately needed a giant can of bug spray," Kaira said.

Lara snorted and Eve smiled.

"Isn't that the truth?" Lara said. "With the StarStorm operational, though, it improves the odds."

Kaira nodded. "It's thanks to you both we have the alliance with the Eon in the first place."

Eve smiled. "Sometimes it's a giant pain in my ass. The Eon king is planning to have a delegation from Earth visit the planet of Eon soon. I'm dreading it."

"Isn't that good news for the alliance?" Kaira said.

"Except I'll have to babysit them." Eve sighed. "A bunch of pretentious politicians from Earth, no doubt."

"You might be too busy giving birth," her sister added.

Eve winced. "Don't talk about giving birth."

Suddenly, the pregnant woman went pale and swayed.

"Eve?" Kaira was closest and grabbed Eve's arm.

"I'm just a little lightheaded. It keeps happening. I just need some space and fresh air."

"You're outside," Lara noted.

"Fresh*er* air. There are too many people."

"I'll take you out front," Kaira said. "There's a small garden there."

"I'll find Davion," Lara said.

Kaira helped the pregnant woman inside and into the elevator.

"I'm feeling better already," Eve said. "I just needed to get away from the crush of people."

Finally, they headed out the front doors of the Woomera main building. There was a small rock garden, with native plants and a metal sculpture, out front.

"Being pregnant with the first Eon-Terran baby is full of surprises," Eve said.

"You're okay now?"

"Yes, but I have an overprotective warrior baby daddy." She glanced at the building. "Uh-oh, incoming."

Kaira saw Davion Thann-Eon striding out the doors, his brows drawn together. He walked like he owned the place. Clearly, a man used to being in charge.

And with him was the sexy silver fox she'd spotted earlier.

Kaira straightened.

The man's gaze met hers and she felt a jolt through her body. He had black eyes crisscrossed with strands of bright green.

"Eve." Davion moved to his mate.

She held up a hand. "I'm fine. Just a bit dizzy, and I needed some air."

The big warrior put his hand on her belly, a tender move. "Let Thane check you over."

221

Thane. Kaira had heard the name. Medical Commander Thane Kann-Eon of the *Rengard.*

As the doctor checked Eve over, he murmured quietly to her.

Davion nodded at Kaira. "Thank you for assisting Eve."

"It was no problem."

"You're fine, Eve," Thane proclaimed. "You just need a little more rest."

Davion let out a gusty sigh. "My mate isn't good at sitting still." He slid his arm around her.

"Your baby is healthy," Thane said.

The couple smiled at each other, then Davion pressed a kiss to Eve's lips.

Kaira moved away to give the couple some privacy. She skirted the metal sculpture and Thane followed her.

"We haven't been introduced. I'm Medical Commander Thane Kann-Eon."

"Commander Kaira Chand. Australia Air Force and head of Woomera Security."

"I'm friends with Sabin. He told me you were excellent to work with."

"That's high praise." She held out her hand.

Thane took it.

As soon as their fingers touched, electricity skated up her arm.

She gasped.

He jolted.

Instant desire flooded Kaira. The green strands in Thane's eyes glowed.

"What the hell?" she breathed. Their fingers twined together.

"Kaira." His voice was deep, guttural. He pulled her close and their bodies collided.

Heat. She felt like flames were licking her. "What's going on?" she whispered.

"I don't know." Thane lowered his head, his hands tightening on her skin. "Can I kiss you, Kaira?"

Her belly clenched. It was what she wanted. More than anything. "Yes."

Then his mouth was on hers firm, hard, and demanding.

The kiss exploded. As their tongues tangled, he pulled her off her feet and she wrapped her legs around his waist. They devoured each other.

"God. *God.*" She bit his bottom lip.

He growled and they writhed against each other. She felt a very sizable bulge rub against her. *Mmm.* Kaira wanted to strip her clothes off, and feel this big warrior move inside her.

"What's happening to us?" she panted.

Suddenly, his black-scale armor flowed over his skin.

"Thane?" She lifted her hands.

He frowned. "I'm not controlling it."

Then, without warning, the scales flowed onto Kaira. Her mouth dropped open.

The armor covered them both.

Their gazes met.

Thane looked shocked. "Instant mating is unheard of."

"Mating?" A crazy mix of emotions churned inside her. "*No. No way.*"

Then, without warning, a Kantos soldier burst out of the darkness.

Hurriedly, Thane set Kaira down and they spun.

A second and third soldier appeared.

Even with the new armor on, it hadn't covered her holstered blaster. She grabbed it and fired.

"Davion, Kantos!" Thane yelled. "Get Eve inside." A long sword formed on Thane's arm.

Kaira and Thane attacked. She fired on the Kantos soldiers, and Thane's sword slammed against another's sharp arms.

Suddenly, something hit Kaira, wrapping around her.

She fell, struggling against the bindings. It was some sort of net made from a sticky brown substance.

"Kaira!"

Thane slashed with his sword and knocked a Kantos back. He ran toward her.

She saw another net hit him. He managed to stay upright, but his sword was trapped against his body. He fought the bindings.

Then the Kantos soldiers were on him. They hit him and Kaira felt a pulse of pain through her body. *No.*

Thane went down. They held up some black substance and slapped it over his wrist. Her scale armor dissolved, and so did his.

A Kantos stepped in front of her, blocking her view. She took in its hard, jointed legs. Then she was lifted and hefted over the alien soldier's shoulder.

She tried to fight, but it was too strong.

The last thing she saw before the Kantos marched into the darkness, were two soldiers carrying a trussed-up and horribly still Thane between them.

Fucking hell. They'd just been abducted by the alien enemy.

———

FINLEY PACED the span of her lab, chewing on a nail and waiting for news.

She reached for her elastic band and realized she wasn't wearing it. She hadn't been since she and Sabin had been abducted. She straightened.

The celebration party had ended abruptly, with the base being locked down. Sabin and the other warriors, along with the security team, had gone to deal with the Kantos.

Everybody knew that Thane and Kaira had been attacked.

Eve sat in a chair nearby, her hand slowly rubbing her belly.

"Are you okay?" Finley asked.

"I'm fine. Dammit, at any other time I could have fought them off." There was frustration in her voice.

"Protecting your child is your number one priority right now."

Eve nodded, but still looked annoyed.

The door opened, and Sabin and Davion entered.

Finley stepped forward. "Kaira? Thane?"

Sabin shook his head. "No sign of them. A small Kantos strike team snatched them and ran."

"Why?" Finley said. "Why take them?"

Davion hugged Eve close. "I suspect they were after me and Eve."

"What?" Eve looked up at him.

"There's some Kantos chatter about them planning to target you."

"And you didn't tell me? The baby." She rested her hand protectively over her belly. "They want our baby."

Davion put his hand over hers. "That's not *ever* going to happen." He lifted his head. "We spoke with King Gayel. The *Desteron* has been tasked with retrieving Commander Chand and Medical Commander Kann-Eon."

"God." Finley went to Sabin, and he hugged her tightly.

"We'll get them back," he said.

"Eve, we need to get back to the *Desteron,* and you need to rest," Davion said. "I want you safe aboard the warship."

She nodded. "Finley, it was a pleasure to meet you. I'm sure we'll see you again soon. We'll keep you updated on your friends."

"Thank you, Eve. Take care."

Sabin and Davion clasped arms, then the couple left.

"Damn the Kantos to hell." Finley kicked her workbench.

"We'll get Kaira and Thane back. For now, we have to focus on the positives. The StarStorm is operational."

"I can't celebrate knowing that the Kantos have Kaira

and Thane." Finley spun away. "Now that the StarStorm is working, I need to focus on detection. We need to figure out a way to stop the small Kantos teams from sneaking onto Earth."

He moved to her and pushed her hair back. "I know that you'll come up with something." He paused. "The *Rengard* is due to leave tomorrow."

Her stomach clenched, like she'd been punched. "You're leaving." Pain stole her breath. She had to be strong. She stared at his chest, blinking back tears.

There was already a hole growing inside her.

"Finley. Finley, look at me."

She did. He touched her cheek, wiping away a tear. Then he gripped her waist and lifted her onto the bench. "I'm not leaving."

"Sabin—" She tried to sort through her feelings. "You're an Eon warrior. How can you stay?"

He gripped her chin. "Because you're my mate. I don't ever want to be without you."

She kissed him, grabbing his shoulders.

"You're mine, Finley Delgado." He bit her bottom lip. "Now and forever."

"I love you, Sabin. To me, you're perfect. You're my everything."

He smiled. "Earlier, I spoke with King Gayel."

Finley swallowed.

"I've been assigned as an Eon ambassador to Earth."

She blinked. "What?"

"I'll work closely with Space Corps. I'll also work closely with my mate to assist her on her projects. I can

227

help upgrade your weapons. And you and I can be together every day."

"Sabin." Love burst through her. "Won't you miss your warship?"

"Maybe. And perhaps one day, we might spend time aboard the *Rengard*. I'd like to take you to meet my family." His hands sank into her hair. "There will be lots of opportunities, and as long as we're together, I'm happy."

"Me, too."

They kissed again and he slid a hand down her body. "You know, I had a few fantasies about you in this lab."

"Really?" She leaned back, basking in the glow of his love. "Why don't you show me?"

He leaned over her. "It will be my pleasure, my sweet Terran mate."

I hope you enjoyed Finley and Sabin's story!

If you're eager to find out the fate of Medical Commander Thane Kann-Eon and Commander Kaira Chand, then you don't have to wait long. Eon Warriors continues with *Soul of Eon*, **releasing next month, February 2021!**

Looking for more action-packed science-fiction romance? **Read on for a preview of *Gladiator*, the first book in Galactic Gladiators.**

Don't miss out! For updates about new releases, action romance info, free books, and other fun stuff, sign up for my VIP mailing list and get your *free box set* containing three action-packed romances.

Visit here to get started: www.annahackett.com

Would you like
a FREE BOX SET
of my books?

PREVIEW: GLADIATOR

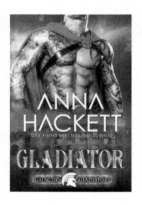

J ust another day at the office.

Harper Adams pulled herself along the outside of the space station module. She could hear her quiet breathing inside her spacesuit, and she easily pulled her weightless body along the slick, white surface of the module. She stopped to check a security panel, ensuring all the systems were running smoothly.

Check. Same as it had been yesterday, and the day

before that. But Harper never ever let herself forget that they were six hundred million kilometers away from Earth. That meant they were dependent only on themselves. She tapped some buttons on the security panel before closing the reinforced plastic cover. She liked to dot all her *I*s and cross all her *T*s. She never left anything to chance.

She grabbed the handholds and started pulling herself up over the cylindrical pod to check the panels on the other side. Glancing back behind herself, she caught a beautiful view of the planet below.

Harper stopped and made herself take it all in. The orange, white, and cream bands of Jupiter could take your breath away. Today, she could even see the famous super-storm of the Great Red Spot. She'd been on the Fortuna Research Station for almost eighteen months. That meant, despite the amazing view, she really didn't see it anymore.

She turned her head and looked down the length of the space station. At the end was the giant circular donut that housed the main living quarters and offices. The main ring rotated to provide artificial gravity for the resi-dents. Lying off the center of the ring was the long cylinder of the research facility, and off that cylinder were several modules that housed various scientific labs and storage. At the far end of the station was the docking area for the supply ships that came from Earth every few months.

"Lieutenant Adams? Have you finished those checks?"

Harper heard the calm voice of her fellow space

marine and boss, Captain Samantha Santos, through the comm system in her helmet.

"Almost done," Harper answered.

"Take a good look at the botany module. The computer's showing some strange energy spikes, but the scientists in there said everything looks fine. Must be a system malfunction."

Which meant the geek squad engineers were going to have to come in and do some maintenance. "On it."

Harper swung her body around, and went feet-first down the other side of the module. She knew the rest of the security team—all made up of United Nations Space Marines—would be running similar checks on the other modules across the station. They had a great team to ensure the safety of the hundreds of scientists aboard the station. There was also a dedicated team of engineers that kept the guts of the station running.

She passed a large, solid window into the module, and could see various scientists floating around benches filled with all kinds of plants. They all wore matching gray jumpsuits accented with bright-blue at the collars, that indicated science team. There was a vast mix of scientists and disciplines aboard—biologists, botanists, chemists, astronomers, physicists, medical experts, and the list went on. All of them were conducting experiments, and some were searching for alien life beyond the edge of the solar system. It seemed like every other week, more probes were being sent out to hunt for radio signals or collect samples.

Since humans had perfected large solar sails as a way to safely and quickly propel spacecraft, getting around the solar system had become a lot easier. With radiation pressure exerted by sunlight onto the mirrored sails, they could travel from Earth to Fortuna Station orbiting Jupiter in just a few months. And many of the scientists aboard the station were looking beyond the solar system, planning manned expeditions farther and farther away. Harper wasn't sure they were quite ready for that.

She quickly checked the adjacent control panel. Among all the green lights, she spotted one that was blinking red, and she frowned. They definitely had a problem with the locking system on the exterior door at the end of the module. She activated the small propulsion pack on her spacesuit, and circled around the module. She slowed down as she passed the large, round exterior door at the end of the cylindrical module.

It was all locked into place and looked secure.

As she moved back to the module, she grabbed a handhold and then tapped the small tablet attached to the forearm of her suit. She keyed in a request for maintenance to come and check it.

She looked up and realized she was right near another window. Through the reinforced glass, a pretty, curvy blonde woman looked up and spotted Harper. She smiled and waved. Harper couldn't help but smile and lifted her gloved hand in greeting.

Dr. Regan Forrest was a botanist and a few years younger than Harper. The young woman was so open and friendly, and had befriended Harper from her first day on the station. Harper had never had a lot of friends —mainly because she'd been too busy raising her younger sister and working. She'd never had time for girly nights out or gossip.

But Regan was friendly, smart, and had the heart of a steamroller under her pretty exterior. Harper always had trouble saying no to her. Maybe the woman reminded her a little of Brianna. At the thought of her sister, something twisted painfully in Harper's chest.

Regan floated over to the window and held up a small tablet. She'd typed in some words.

Cards tonight?

Harper had been teaching Regan how to play poker. The woman was terrible at it, and Harper beat her all the time. But Regan never gave up.

Harper nodded and held up two fingers to indicate a couple of hours. She was off-shift shortly, and then she had a sparring match with Regan's cousin, Rory—one of the station engineers—in the gym. Aurora "Call me Rory or I'll hit you" Fraser had been trained in mixed martial arts, and Harper found the female engineer a hell of a sparring partner. Rory was teaching Harper some martial arts moves and Harper was showing the woman some basic sword moves. Since she was little, Harper had been a keen fencer.

Regan grinned back and nodded. Then the woman's wide smile disappeared. She spun around, and through the glass Harper could see the other scientists all looking around, concerned. One scientist was spinning around, green plants floating in the air around him, along with fat droplets of water and some other green fluid. He'd clearly screwed up and let his experiment get free.

"Lieutenant Adams?" The captain's voice came through her helmet again. "Harper?"

There was a sense of urgency that made Harper's belly tighten. "Go ahead, Captain."

"We have an alarm sounding in the botany module. The computer says there is a risk of decompression."

Dammit. "I just checked the security panels. The locking mechanism on the exterior door is showing red. I did a visual inspection and it's closed up tight."

"Okay, we talked with the scientist in charge. Looks like one of her team let something loose in there. It isn't dangerous, but it must be messing with the alarm sensors. System's locked them all in there." She made an annoyed sound. "Idiots will have to stay there until engineering can get down there and free them."

Harper studied the room through the glass again. Some of the green liquid had floated over to another bench that contained various frothing cylinders on it. A second later, the cylinders shattered, their contents bubbling upward.

The scientists all moved to the back exit of the module, banging on the locked door. *Damn.* They were trapped.

Harper met Regan's gaze. Her friend's face was pale, and wisps of her blonde hair had escaped her ponytail, floating around her face.

"Captain," Harper said. "Something's wrong. The experiments have overflowed their containment." She could see the scientists were all coughing.

"Engineering is on the way," the captain said.

Harper pushed herself off, flying over the surface of

the module. She reached the control panel and saw that several other lights had turned red. They needed to get this under control and they needed to do it now.

"Harper!" The captain's panicked voice. "Decompression in progress!"

What the hell? The module jerked beneath Harper. She looked up and saw the exterior door blow off, flying away from the station.

Her heart stopped. That meant all the scientists were exposed to the vacuum of space.

Fuck. Harper pushed off again, sending herself flying toward the end of the module. She put her arms by her sides to help increase her speed. Through the window, she saw that most of the scientists had grabbed on to whatever they could hold on to. A few were pulling emergency breathers over their heads.

She reached the end of the pod and saw the damage. There was torn metal where the door had been ripped off. Inside the door, she knew there would be a temporary repair kit containing a sheet of high-tech nano fabric that could be stretched across the opening to reestablish pressure. But it needed to be put in place manually. Harper reached for the latch to release the repair kit.

Suddenly, a slim body shot out of the pod, her arms and legs kicking. Her mouth was wide open in a silent scream.

Regan. Harper didn't let herself think. She turned, pushed off and fired her propulsion system, arrowing after her friend.

"Security Team to the botany module," she yelled through her comm system. "Security Team to botany module. We have decompression. One scientist has been expelled. I'm going after her. I need someone that can help calm the others and get the module sealed again."

"Acknowledged, Lieutenant," Captain Santos answered. "I'm on my way."

Harper focused on reaching Regan. She was gaining on her. She saw that the woman had lost consciousness. She also knew that Regan had only a couple of minutes to survive out here. Harper let her training take over. She tapped the propulsion system controls, trying for more speed, as she maneuvered her way toward Regan.

As she got close, Harper reached out and wrapped her arm around the scientist. "I've got you."

Harper turned, at the same time clipping a safety line to the loops on Regan's jumpsuit. Then, she touched the controls and propelled them straight back towards the module. She kept her friend pulled tightly toward her chest. *Hold on, Regan.*

She was so still. It reminded Harper of holding Brianna's dead body in her arms. Harper's jaw tightened. She wouldn't let Regan die out here. The woman had dreamed of working in space, and worked her entire career to get here, even defying her family. Harper wasn't going to fail her.

As the module got closer, she saw that the security team had arrived. She saw the captain's long, muscled body as she and another man put up the nano fabric.

"Incoming. Keep the door open."

"Can't keep it open much longer, Adams," the captain replied. "Make it snappy."

Harper adjusted her course, and, a second later, she

shot through the door with Regan in her arms. Behind her, the captain and another huge security marine, Lieutenant Blaine Strong, pulled the stretchy fabric across the opening.

"Decompression contained," the computer intoned.

Harper released a breath. On the panel beside the door, she saw the lights turning green. The nano fabric wouldn't hold forever, but it would do until they got everyone out of here, and then got a maintenance team in here to fix the door.

"Oxygen levels at required levels," the computer said again.

"Good work, Lieutenant." Captain Sam Santos floated over. She was a tall woman with a strong face and brown hair she kept pulled back in a tight ponytail. She had curves she kept ruthlessly toned, and golden skin she always said was thanks to her Puerto Rican heritage.

"Thanks, Captain." Harper ripped her helmet off and looked down at Regan.

Her blonde hair was a wild tangle, her face was pale and marked by what everyone who worked in space called space hickeys—bruises caused by the skin's small blood vessels bursting when exposed to the vacuum of space. *Please be okay.*

"Here." Blaine appeared, holding a portable breather. The big man was an excellent marine. He was about six foot five with broad shoulders that stretched his spacesuit to the limit. She knew he was a few inches over the height limit for space operations, but he was a damn good marine, which must have gone in his favor. He had dark skin thanks to his African-American father and his handsome face made him popular with the station's single ladies, but mostly he worked and hung out with the other marines.

"Thanks." Harper slipped the clear mask over Regan's mouth.

"Nice work out there." Blaine patted her shoulder. "She's alive because of you."

Suddenly, Regan jerked, pulling in a hard breath.

"You're okay." Harper gripped Regan's shoulder. "Take it easy."

Regan looked around the module, dazed and panicky. Harper watched as Regan caught sight of the fabric stretched across the end of the module, and all the plants floating around inside.

"God," Regan said with a raspy gasp, her breath fogging up the dome of the breather. She shook her head, her gaze moving to Harper. "Thanks, Harper."

"Any time." Harper squeezed her friend's shoulder. "It's what I'm here for."

Regan managed a wan smile. "No, it's just you. You didn't have to fly out into space to rescue me. I'm grateful."

"Come on. We need to get you to the infirmary so they can check you out. Maybe put some cream on your hickeys."

"Hickeys?" Regan touched her face and groaned. "Oh, no. I'm going to get a ribbing."

"And you didn't even get them the pleasurable way."

A faint blush touched Regan's cheeks. "That's right. If I had, at least the ribbing would have been worth it."

With a relieved laugh, Harper looked over at her captain. "I'm going to get Regan to the infirmary."

The other woman nodded. "Good. We'll meet you back at the Security Center."

With a nod, Harper pushed off, keeping one arm around Regan, and they floated into the main part of the science facility. Soon, they moved through the entrance into the central hub of the space station. As the artificial gravity hit, Harper's boots thudded onto the floor. Beside her, Regan almost collapsed.

Harper took most of the woman's weight and helped her down the corridor. They pushed into the infirmary.

A gray-haired, barrel-chested man rushed over. "Decided to take an unscheduled spacewalk, Dr. Forrest?"

Regan smiled weakly. "Yes. Without a spacesuit."

The doctor made a tsking sound and then took her from Harper. "We'll get her all patched up."

Harper nodded. "I'll come and check on you later."

Regan grabbed her hand. "We have a blackjack game scheduled. I'm planning to win back all those chocolates you won off me."

Harper snorted. "You can try." It was good to see some life back in Regan's blue eyes.

As Harper strode out into the corridor, she ran a hand through her dark hair, tension slowly melting out of her shoulders. She really needed a beer. She tilted her neck one way and then the other, hearing the bones pop.

Just another day at the office. The image of Regan drifting away from the space station burst in her head.

Harper released a breath. She was okay. Regan was safe and alive. That was all that mattered.

With a shake of her head, Harper headed toward the Security Center. She needed to debrief with the captain and clock off. Then she could get out of her spacesuit and take the one-minute shower that they were all allotted.

That was the one thing she missed about Earth. Long, hot showers.

And swimming. She'd been a swimmer all her life and there were days she missed slicing through the water.

She walked along a long corridor, meeting a few people—mainly scientists. She reached a spot where there was a long bank of windows that afforded a lovely view of Jupiter, and space beyond it.

Stingy showers and unscheduled spacewalks aside, Harper had zero regrets about coming out into space. There'd been nothing left for her on Earth, and to her surprise, she'd made friends here on Fortuna.

As she stared out into the black, mesmerized by the twinkle of stars, she caught a small flash of light in the distance. She paused, frowning. What the hell was that?

She stared hard at the spot where she'd seen the flash. Nothing there but the pretty sprinkle of stars. Harper shook her head. Fatigue was playing tricks on her. It had to have just been a weird trick of the lights reflecting off the glass.

Pushing the strange sighting away, she continued on to the Security Center.

Galactic Gladiators
Gladiator

Warrior
Hero
Protector
Champion
Barbarian
Beast
Rogue
Guardian
Cyborg
Imperator
Hunter
Also Available as Audiobooks!

ALSO BY ANNA HACKETT

Unidentified

Undetected

Also Available as Audiobooks!

Eon Warriors

Edge of Eon

Touch of Eon

Heart of Eon

Kiss of Eon

Mark of Eon

Claim of Eon

Storm of Eon

Also Available as Audiobooks!

Galactic Gladiators: House of Rone

Sentinel

Defender

Centurion

Paladin

Guard

Weapons Master

Also Available as Audiobooks!

Galactic Gladiators

Gladiator

Warrior

Hero

Protector

Champion

Barbarian

Beast

Rogue

Guardian

Cyborg

Imperator

Hunter

Also Available as Audiobooks!

Hell Squad

Marcus

Cruz

Gabe

Reed

Roth

Noah

Shaw

Holmes

Niko

Finn

Theron

Hemi

On a Barbarian World

Lost in Barbarian Space

Through Uncharted Space

Crashed on an Ice World

Perma Series

Winter Fusion

A Galactic Holiday

Warriors of the Wind

Tempest

Storm & Seduction

Fury & Darkness

Standalone Titles

Savage Dragon

Hunter's Surrender

One Night with the Wolf

For more information visit www.annahackett.com

ABOUT THE AUTHOR

I'm a USA Today bestselling romance author who's passionate about *fast-paced, emotion-filled* contemporary and science fiction romance. I love writing about people overcoming unbeatable odds and achieving seemingly impossible goals. I like to believe it's possible for all of us to do the same.

I live in Australia with my own personal hero and two very busy, always-on-the-move sons.

For release dates, behind-the-scenes info, free books, and other fun stuff, sign up for the latest news here:

Website: www.annahackett.com